THE LAST GIFT

and other tales

Mary Rothwell

SCRIPTORA

Published in Great Britain 2021

by

SCRIPTORA
25 Summerhill Road, London N15

in association with SWWJ
(Society of Women Writers & Journalists)
www.swwj.co.uk

ISBN: 978-0-9500591-7-4

Printed and bound by Witley Press
Hunstanton PE36 6AD
www.witleypress.co.uk

ACKNOWLEDGEMENTS

Thanks are due to the Hastings Writers' Group for prizes awarded to the following stories:

"Paradise" – 1st prize Catherine Cookson Cup

"Family Tree" – 3rd prize Catherine Cookson Cup

"Life Changes" – shortlisted for Catherine Cookson Cup

And to *Strandline* for publishing the following:

Vol 2 "After"

Vol 3 "John the Pump"

Vol 4 "Life Changes"

Vol 5 "Think Rainbow"

Vol 6 "Spider in a Bottle"

Vol 7 "Snakes and Ladders"

Thanks are also due to the late lamented *Illiterati* writers for their positive feedback on a number of these stories and also to SWWJ judges for applauding the stories entered in their competitions, in particular "Out of Touch" and "An Afternoon in the Park".

Cover design: Jasmine Lapper-Goodrum

In memory of Leila Davies and of Maurice Lester

CONTENTS

THE LAST GIFT

A sports bag over one shoulder, he set off each morning about ten, as soon as he'd read the *Guardian* and seen to the dog. On hot days he wore sandals, faded shorts and a tee-shirt. He favoured red or red and black. And sunglasses, of course. He would walk along the promenade as far as the pier, then strike inland for a black coffee at the *Pig*, or a pint at *French's*. Then on to the Old Town to see what bargains he could pick up. He sometimes spent several hours browsing, conversing with the proprietors and other book lovers, increasing his already wide knowledge of the world in general. Thence to the *Pump House* or the *Anchor Inn* for a final coffee before turning westward again, reaching home between five and six, in time for supper.

Rachel knows all this because, in the early days of his redundancy, Davy used to telephone her every evening. She always asked, out of politeness, how he'd spent his day and he, she presumed also out of politeness, would tell her. These days he telephones her less often, but occasionally they meet, by accident, on the promenade, in the late afternoon. Sometimes, whilst waiting for the bus to her job at the antiquarian bookshop, Rachel glimpses him plodding resolutely towards the pier. It is always just after ten, so she knows he is keeping to the timetable he has set himself.

Latterly, due to the unwelcome attentions Jen, Rachel's Labrador, has been receiving from a Rottweiler in the park, they take their afternoon walk on the beach instead. At low-tide, Jen will pound over the hot sand chasing seagulls, splash about in the shallows, sniff out shellfish on the edges of rock pools. At high-tide, they are driven inland on to the narrow concrete of the lower promenade and forced to exercise in a straight line; so far west to east, turn, then back again east to west, scooping poops as they go.

Often on these walks, they rest awhile on one of the alcove seats lining the promenade. Occasionally, Davy joins them. Jen lies panting on the cool stone, her head flat on his sandalled foot, adoring eyes fixed on his face.

Rachel and he begin to talk again, as of old. But he is more critical of things, denigrating television programmes, scorning new films that interest her. Their discussions, formerly deep and satisfying, now tend almost to shallowness and peter out after a few minutes. But on personal matters he is as generous as ever. Every time they meet he presents her with a gift. Unzipping one end of his sports bag, he pulls out some treasure he's picked up for a song. Shyly, he offers it to her.

'Look. I found this for you.'

'What is it?'

'What is it? It's a wok, of course. For your vegetarian meals.'

'Thank you.'

Other times it is a set of soufflé dishes, a blue china teapot, a butterfly brooch, a bunch of paperbacks. She feels overwhelmed by and resentful of these presents which she doesn't really want. The books especially, because, by their subject matter, history and biographies, she guesses he really chose them for himself. Also, the condition of a book, the touch and smell of it, does not seem to interest him in the least, only the information within.

In July her job comes to an end. She returns to the dole, struggles to pay bills, skips lunch.

'Don't worry,' he comforts her, 'I'll look after you.'

'But you're on the dole too.'

'Still got my treasure chest, haven't I?' He pats the side of his nose.

Vaguely she remembers an old box under his bed. In former days she has delighted in rummaging through it. There was a silver tin, a porcelain figurine, a small telescope and a worn leather pouch whose contents she never discovered.

'When I go, that's yours. All of it.'

'What do you mean, go?'

But he will not say. Just touches his nose with two fingers and winks at her.

'Anyway, it's locked.'

'You know where the key is.'

'No, I don't.'

'You remember? Willy Wagdagger.'

'Willy? Your little dog?'

He smiles now, almost laughs. For a second, the man she once loved is returned in all his fullness before her. The next moment he has vanished and she is once more dealing with a stranger.

Watching him, she says to herself I used to make love to that body. I remember curling into its heat on cold winter nights, ruffling its pelt. For he is covered all over with soft, blond hair. She knows him, both inside and out. She knows, for instance, that he wears dark glasses summer and winter, not because of weak eyes as he claims, not to protect them from the light, but from people's gaze. Without them, he feels exposed and frightened, then awkward about that too. As for the outsize sports bag he now carries with him everywhere, she guesses it is to accommodate an old friend he has rediscovered, one who makes no emotional demands. She guesses also that his evening accounts of his activities are regularly omitting his daily visits to the off-licence in town.

She suspects he's not eating properly and challenges him on this.

'Don't worry about me. You look after yourself' is his response.

He is growing thinner, his face is older than it should be, his hair receding faster.

'I've run out of pain-killers.'

'What pain-killers?'

'The ones the doctor gave me.'

'What for?'

'My pain, of course.'

He is irritated, his voice on edge.

'He's sending me for a scan. It's a waste of time.'

'Don't say that.'

'I might not go anyway.'

Blue and golden cans, sextuplets joined at the neck; from throats to throat the golden liquid flows, bittersweet and heavy as syrup, it fills the aching hollow, relieves all responsibilities, dulls all pain.

Rachel observes him from the upper promenade as he ambles homeward, face into the sun. The bag on his back bulges with cans, is as heavy as a child, more faithful than a dog. He does not see her.

He is on the last run. Instinctively she knows this and can do nothing.

In the kitchen, the lino has been wrenched off. A roll of new chequered vinyl, black and white, leans against the refrigerator; there's crumpled newspaper, a splat of Pedigree Chum, the smell of dog poo.

He wakes in the night, fumbles for switches, misses them, stumbles out onto the newspaper, leans forward in the darkness, desperate for the lavatory. Somehow a rod of white-hot steel is branding his back, screwing into it. He's amazed he cannot smell the flesh burning. He's in the bathroom, losing direction, cursing the tangle of jump leads he meant to deliver to Nick yesterday. He trips, the steel rod stakes him to the floor, his bladder lets go and he is still falling. 'Oh, hell,' he screams in a whisper.

So Rachel imagines when she finds him there, still and cold, embroiled in the jump leads like Medusa with her snakes, stale urine and vomit coating his furry body, and the little dog whining piteously.

She has not seen him for three days. He did not answer when she telephoned. Reluctantly, she ascended the familiar stairs, slipped the latch, entered his once-immaculate flat. It is a tip.

Stale beer, doggy scent, accumulated grime, mouldering food, the potage of smells catches at her throat. She retches, swallows hard. Automatically, she starts to clear away the shit and rubbish in the kitchen. Half an hour later she remembers there is a dead body behind the bathroom door and she must do something. She telephones his sister who will be along in an hour or so. Rachel is exhorted to touch nothing. Edna is an accountant and so counts things. She has an excellent memory and knows where all his possessions are. Her meaning is plain.

Rachel takes the kettle from the hob, sees the congealed mountain of crockery covering the sink and draining board and puts it back. She will not think about that thing in there being Davy or she will cry. Not yet, not yet, she tells herself fiercely. She strokes the dog's bony spine. Willy licks her hand, his eyes full of longing. Absently, she opens a fresh tin of meat for him.

Suddenly she remembers the treasure chest. Wading through a field of dirty clothes, empty cans and fish and chip papers, she reaches the bed, kneels on the sticky carpet, pulls out the box. The little dog runs to her side, tail wagging. She unscrews the capsule attached to his collar which is supposed to contain his address. A tiny key drops out. She unlocks the box. It is now empty save for a small, leather-bound book. A swift intake of breath and it is couched in her hands. Its yellow leaves smell of autumn. She holds it to her nose, breathes in its skin, her mind already breathing in the well-loved words.

Wordsworth's 'Prelude'. Could it be a first edition?

Brisk footsteps echo on the bare wooden stairs, a banister creaks ominously. The dog barks. Rachel stuffs book and key into her shoulder bag. The box smells of parchment and pipe tobacco. Gently she closes the lid and slides it back under the bed.

****

SOMETHING FROM NOTHING

When Manny Goodman married Clare Sanderson, who was five years younger than his eldest son and the same age as his only daughter, not one of his family came to the ceremony. Not even his brother David who had been his best friend for as long as he could remember.

'Why couldn't you find a nice Jewish girl? If you really had to marry again,' he complained.

'You sound just like Mother! I married Rebecca, didn't I? God rest her soul. Four sons and a daughter. I've done my duty.'

'No good will come of it,' David moaned on, 'you mark my words. Age, religion, custom; you've got nothing in common.'

But Manny didn't care. He'd loved her from the first moment he saw her standing by the open window of his partner's office. The curve of her shoulder beneath a silken blouse, and when she turned, the lift of a firm breast. An errant breeze stirring smooth, dark hair.

He guessed he must have caught her in a rare moment of daydreaming for she had started at his entrance, the sober little face blushing becomingly. He'd obtained Bernard's signatures and returned reluctantly to his own middle-aged secretary. All that afternoon, his heart had skipped and jumped alarmingly.

Their courtship had been surprisingly swift and easy. Although she didn't have to marry him. He'd made that quite plain. He wasn't seeking another Rebecca.

'But I love you, Manny. I want to be your wife,' she had whispered.

The registrar's office was filled with Clare's cousins and aunts and uncles. Her parents put on a lavish reception. There was gold leaf on all the candles on all the tables and orchids in the cut glass vases. Champagne flowed freely. It was a thoroughly Gentile occasion. Not a yarmulke in sight. And thick cream on the desserts.

Their honeymoon in the Seychelles was blissful. They returned to his Hampstead house, moving temporarily into the guest suite. To his relief, she gave up her job and proved to be as skilled at running their home as she had been Bernard's office. And to Manny's joy, she proved wiser than Rebecca by never once trying to run him.

Manny had bowled into marriage on a roller-coaster of delight, questioning nothing. Only now, six months later, were doubts beginning to surface. What could she see in him? Fifty-three, hair greying, though blessedly not yet thinning too much, an infant paunch and a taste for oysters and other rich food which his doctor tried in vain to scare him out of.

Also, he worked long hours. He got a kick out of making money and enjoyed spending it too. His family considered this his only possible attraction for a twenty-three-year-old young woman. But Manny knew that Clare was rich in her own right. She didn't need his money.

Yet his doubts refused to die. He found himself watching her, as he used to do before she was his. The frequency of their love-making had not lessened but it was calmer. Now she seemed to make love almost absent-mindedly, often gazing at some invisible thing beyond his left shoulder. He missed the passionate little body pressing like a hard knot against his chest or sinuous beneath him, legs clasped across his back.

His brother's words haunted him and the more he analysed, the greater his doubts grew. Thirty years of life and experience separated them. What was there to bind them?

This morning, he'd reached out for her only to see her slip, wraith-like from the bed and his hand grasping air.

'Not now, Manny. It's nearly eight. Bagel time!' She loved to tease him with his own sayings.

When he reached the kitchen, he found smoked haddock swimming in butter on the table and Clare already eating.

'I'm starving, Manny!' And she cut herself a doorstep of bread.

'You'll put on weight.'

'Not me. I'm as thin as a rake.'

He did not need to look at her to know that this was no longer true. She was growing more curvaceous daily, much to his gratification.

'Oh, by the way, I've managed to get tickets for the Mozart concert next week.'

'Darling! You spoil me.'

'I shall enjoy it too, you know.'

He gulped coffee, picked up his briefcase. She called after him. 'I'm going out this evening.'

Direct as ever. 'Where?' he asked, heart jumping a little.

'Only to the gym.'

She had told him about aerobics but he'd thought they were afternoon classes. Was there some handsome youth in the evenings, all bronzed and muscular? He paused on his way through the hall, sideways to the long mirror, lifting his chin and straining on recalcitrant stomach muscles.

At the front door, she ran up to kiss him goodbye, warm arms round his neck and lips all buttery. A sweet pain in his heart. Gently he disentangled himself.

'Shall I leave you a salad?'

'No. Don't worry. I'll go round to David's.'

He could not bear to return to the house and she not be in it.

He did not, however, go immediately to his brother's for supper, as he had implied. Instead, he grabbed a quick sandwich at a station buffet. To arrive, unannounced and alone for supper? He could imagine Miriam's raised eyebrows, the careful questions.

It was gone eight when he finally arrived in Highgate. Miriam opened the door.

'He's up in the attic. With his latest toy. I've barely seen him for days.'

All his life, David had gone from craze to craze. Each new activity was what he'd always been searching for. Until the next interest caught him.

'What's it this time?'

'You'll soon find out.' She then changed tack abruptly as he'd noticed women often did. 'How's that young wife of yours?'

'Fine. Fine.'

'Happy …?

'… Yes, very, thank …'

'... or a little moody?'

Manny looked at her sharply but she only smiled. 'You best go on up the stairs. And', she warned in mock sombre tones, 'knock before you enter.'

The attic landing was crowded with new shelves, and they with jugs and bottles of all sorts. On a line strung across the banisters were pegged several large black and white photographs.

He knocked on the attic door. It opened immediately, white light flooding out. Then David's bulk blocked it. Without a word, they hugged.

'So? How's married life, then?'

'I've done it before, remember.'

'Happy?'

'Very.'

David punched his shoulder affectionately.

'Come into my cave. See where miracles are wrought.'

Manny had never felt the need to capture images, not even, so far, Clare's. His memory was vivid enough, too sharp sometimes. David led him into his darkroom, flicking switches as he went. The white light was replaced by a rosy glow. The room became a grotto and Manny could make out very little.

'I've just done a test strip for this one,' said David, placing a negative in a little drawer at the top of an enlarger. 'Twenty seconds should be about right.'

He laid a large sheet of mottled paper on a baseboard, turned on the enlarger and counted to twenty. When the lamp went off, the shadowy images disappeared. He took the apparently blank paper and slid it into the first of three trays where it floated like a dead leaf on a pond.

'There's nothing on it,' puzzled Manny. 'You can't make a picture from nothing.'

'Yes, you can. Nothing …'

'… doesn't even exist!' interrupted Manny.

'Quite right. But there is always something, only if we're not aware of it, we say there is nothing.'

'To conceal our ignorance?'

'To name the unnameable.'

'Okay. As far as I can see, that page is blank. Better?'

'Better.' He nudged the tray and the liquid swirled gently. 'It's all a matter of chemistry. Look!'

Almost imperceptibly a dark curl began to appear. As if a thumbnail were piercing a white blind. Manny watched, fascinated. The curl became a thin curve which flowed into bands of light and shade which in turn draped themselves around a body. His heart jumped in that scary way it had when he saw her first.

'Clare! It's Clare! How? When?'

He turned almost accusingly to his brother.

'The firm's Christmas party. Remember?'

Of course. David, scouting round with his new camera, had come upon them in Manny's office. Clare's head was turned, her eyes directly challenging the camera. It was an excellent likeness.

On impulse, Manny declined David's offer of a lift and walked home, cutting across a corner of the Heath. Risky, but it wasn't far. It was a windless night and mild for March. Above, a new moon in a sea of stars, encircled the shadow of the old moon. Grounded with him were armies of daffodils and crocuses where only a few weeks ago had been nothing but bare earth. He walked slowly, feeling as if he were seeing it all for the first time. A fluttering of hope gathered strength and gradually rooted in his heart. All would be well. He would believe this.

His house was ablaze with light. He could hear the music from the end of the drive. The Jupiter! His favourite. He opened the front door and a flushed Clare ran into his arms.

'Are we having a party? Did I forget?'

She bowed her head. 'It's just …' A swift intake of breath. '… I don't like it at night when you're not here.'

He thought he understood. 'Ghosts?'

Manny himself was daily reminded of Rebecca in this house, even though they had moved into the guest suite. The oak panelling, the brown paintwork, the discreet lighting. Too many memories. Perhaps they should move. He would think about it.

They sat down on the old sofa, Mozart coming to a climax behind them. She curled into his arms and he was reminded of the new moon embracing the old.

'Who is it you see over my shoulder?' He asked into her hair.

'Mmmh?'

‘That serene gaze of yours, when I’m loving you?’

‘Oh, just thinking.’

‘Thinking?’

‘I’m wondering …’ She curled in closer to him. ‘I wonder if he’ll look like you. Or like me.’

‘Who?’

‘Our son, of course!’

He couldn’t speak. The possibility had somehow never occurred to him. But Miriam had suspected. Women’s intuition. It never failed to astonish him. He sent up a silent prayer to Jehovah or Jesus or whoever it was who arranged these things. Something could and always would come from what men called nothing. Nothing in his case had been falling in love with the curve of a shoulder.

Just chemistry, David had said, but to Manny it was a miracle. All of it. A beautiful miracle.

****

THE REINDEER

It was a cold November morning, two weeks before Christmas, when Richard set out on his weekly walk to the town centre. He'd chosen the promenade route because the sea always fascinated him. He never tired of watching the play of light upon the water. He felt something inside him rejoice at the thunder of the waves as they crashed onto the shingle.

Young Josy had loved it too, squealing delightedly when the sea chased her up the beach, and those grey eyes, so like his own, wide with wonder.

Down on the lower promenade, on rough days like today, it was so noisy that conversation with his friend George was just impossible. But George wasn't here anymore either. Richard had to keep reminding himself of this.

As he turned the corner by the cafe, the full force of the wind caught him and he was very glad of the gabardine coat his friend had bequeathed him.

'My best coat, it's in the wardrobe,' George had implored him, as the ambulance men were strapping him into the chair.

'You won't need that in hospital.'

'It's for you, you old fool. The Social will come and clear everything out. I want you to have it.'

'But you'll be home in a few days.'

'No. I shan't be needing it again.'

'George?'

'Goodbye Richie. You've been a good friend to me.'

And that was that.

It was a dark blue coat with a quilted lining and lots of pockets. Over the years, he and George had shrunk to much the same size and the coat fitted him like a glove. He pulled it closer, fastening its belt against the gale. It felt good to have something of George's with him.

Being old was bad enough, now he was alone again as well. It was already a year since his son, Jack, had got that job up north and taken young Josy with him.

'Dad, she's missing her mother. And Wendy's parents have offered to look after her while I'm at work. We'll come and see you, and you can always phone,' Jack had reassured him.

But the promises had remained promises and if he were to telephone the little girl one evening from a draughty phone booth carpeted with fag-ends and decorated with foul graffiti, what would he say to her?

As he was passing the pier, he noticed that Christmas lights were being put up. And, at the square, a huge Christmas tree was already in place.

'They start Christmas so early these days,' he muttered half to himself.

‘So they have more time to get money out of you,’ said a voice nearby.

A green-coated bundle of a woman was shuffling past him. Richard caught the acrid whiff of unwashed flesh and edged away. But he saw that her eyes were robin-bright, and her voice, low and insistent, held him against his will.

‘Santa’s coming here tomorrow,’ she offered.

‘Santa?’ said Richard.

‘That bloke in red. You know,’ she scorned. ‘On a sleigh pulled by real live reindeers brought down special from a mountain in Scotland.’

‘What time?’ Richard asked politely, not really caring. What had Santa, or Christmas for that matter, to do with him?

‘There’s a poster behind you.’ she pointed with a grimy finger, then answered before he could get out his glasses and read it.

‘Two o’clock. And there’s brass bands and majorettes too.’

Richard, even when George was alive, would normally come into the town centre only once a week, to collect his pension and buy a lottery ticket. He realised the woman was expecting an answer. ‘Oh, I don’t really think - ‘

‘Ah, go on, it’ll be a lark,’ she coaxed. ‘I never seed a real reindeer before.’

Richard was suddenly aware that he hadn’t either but didn’t want to admit it. As the crowds jostled them, he managed to move away from her. If Josy were with him, he’d come tomorrow. It would be worth it just to see those grey eyes shining.

The queue at the post office was long. So was the one at the lottery counter. By the time he came out, he was aching to sit down somewhere. He considered going for a mug of tea at Phil's cafe, but then he'd need the toilets and they were on the far side of the centre in the opposite direction of home.

He looked about desperately. There was nothing. Then he remembered an old brick wall where he and George used to sit sometimes. It was round the corner of the little theatre, in a back street behind the brand-new shopping centre. The forgotten part of town, where old things were still allowed to be old. It was out of the wind and ran parallel with a newer, concrete wall which neatly provided a support to lean against.

He settled himself here and rolled a cigarette, a precious treat these days. He was well into an imaginary conversation with George when he heard a sound behind him. It was an odd sound which he half-recognized.

Peering over his shoulder, he realised for the first time exactly where these walls were. They bounded the old milk yard where he used to play as a boy: the setts which sloped to a central drain where huge puddles formed on rainy days, the big shed full of milk floats, clanging churns, a stable for the horses. It had been a place of endless fascination.

He must have dreamed that munching sound. There were no horses now. The milk yard had been derelict for years. But there, in the shadows, something had definitely moved. With difficulty, Richard hauled his legs over the wall and approached the old stable. At first, he could see nothing, so he eased himself round the door and was instantly enveloped in the rough scent of warm hay.

A gentle snuffling at his elbow and he found himself gazing into liquid brown eyes beneath candelabra antlers. Astonished, he instinctively offered his hand for inspection. The reindeer rubbed his nose softly against it and did not back off.

Richard stroked the velvety snout, patted the warm flank, laid his arm over the unresisting back, and was utterly content. His eyes shone and his lips parted in a smile of pure wonder. So they stayed in close and companionable stillness until the door banged open and a sharp voice called out.

'Who are you? What are you doing here? These aren't pets, you know!'

Richard did not like confrontation, so he mumbled something indecipherable and slipped past the man without explanation. But all the way home, he kept his hand curled inside his pocket, couching the memory of the reindeer's touch, keeping it alive for as long as he could.

The following morning, he was woken abruptly from a dream in which he was a child again, grooming Bathsheba, the white pony on his grandfather's farm. He could feel the warmth of the animal's neck under his hands, hear its gentle contented breathing.

Down in the road, a hooter tore at the frosty air. Dragging on trousers, he peered round the curtain. A large, green lorry was parking up outside. Richard hobbled across his bedroom, struggling into shoes and a sweater, then went as fast as he could down the stairs and into the street.

'Hi Dad,' called Jack, hugging him. 'Had a delivery near here so thought I'd pop over and see you. Of course, as soon as I told Josy …'

'Josy?' said Richard, hardly daring to hope.

As Jack reached up to open the cab door, Richard was right beside him. An excited squeal, a flurry of yellow hair and she was falling into his arms.

'Grampie!'

Over her bobbing head, he met his son's eyes.

'How long can you stay?'

'Couple of nights. If you can put us up.'

'Of course.'

Then to Josy.

'I've got a special treat for you today.'

****

JOHN THE PUMP

This story is a 'faction', neither entirely fact nor entirely fiction. The events in the childhood of Johann Sebastian Bach are imagined but he was undoubtedly a great composer and the music named was all definitely his work.

He was only just nine, but he had proved that day that he could do the work of older boys. His feet and hands, their skin broken by the rough stalks, smarted badly, but he hadn't cared. Heavy in the pocket of his grubby breeches jingled the six pennies the farmer had paid him. And stuffed into the other pocket was the package the farmer's wife had thrust at him as he passed her kitchen door.

It had been hard work and a long day. The men cut the oats first, at sunrise, while the dew was still on them. Then, after a breakfast of bacon and bread washed down with weak beer, they started on the corn. The toothed edges of their sickles slapped through the stalks with a zinging sound. Behind, came the boys, gathering up the corn in their arms to tie it into sheaves.

The sun was still hot on his aching back as he trotted down the lane past the church. From time to time, he glanced warily over his shoulder, but could see no one. On impulse, he entered the churchyard, perched on a gravestone, and laid out the day's treasures. First the pennies, hot and sticky, and still a smudge of his blood on one of them, then a tin whistle he'd found in a hedgerow, and lastly, the package from the farmer's wife.

Cautiously, he unknotted the crude napkin, then gasped in delight. There was a slice of game pie, a hunk of cheese, and a pinky golden fruit he didn't know the name of. His stomach contracted just at the sight of such a feast. The farmer had given the men sausage and beer at five o'clock, but the boys had to be satisfied with a mug of milk and whatever they could beg from the men. For one second, he thought to take the food home, but knew it wouldn't go far round the table with his many brothers and sisters.

The next second, he'd wolfed half the pie, and in five minutes he was scraping up the crumbs. The golden fruit had gone down with the rest, its juice both sharp and sweet. The stone in its middle, he put in his pocket for later. He wiped his mouth with the back of his hand and was packing away his remaining treasures when the crackling of twigs amongst the trees caught his attention. Instantly he was alert, his body tensed, ready to run.

'He came this way, I'm sure of it,' a boy's voice from below the churchyard wall.

He ducked down out of sight. It was Thomas and his gang after his pennies. If only he'd gone straight home, they'd never have caught up with him. He'd be safe on his stool by the fire or helping his mother with the little ones. There was only a hawthorn bush between him and the gang. Crouching low, he dodged from grave to grave until he found himself at the door of the church, which stood ajar. He slipped like a shadow into the vestibule. Straining at the great iron latch, he pushed the door shut behind him. It clanged like an out of tune bell.

It was cold there, after the sunlight. His thin shirt, sweat-soaked and torn was little comfort. He shivered. Suddenly there came a loud sound, from inside the church. Curious yet apprehensive, he opened the inner door and slid from darkness into the soft, yellow candlelit interior. It came again, a long drawn-out, deep orange sound which soared to the rafters, and clung there and sung there, till it slowly faded and died. Soon after, he heard a clattering up above, as of wood on wood. He half-expected to see clog dancers, but the sound was slightly muffled as if their shoes were decorated with felt.

He crept up the aisle, his bare feet silent on the smooth flagstones. He wrinkled his nose at the dusty scent of the stone pillars he passed. A familiar acrid smell of candle grease reminded him of where he should be and he turned suddenly. At that same moment, he sensed movement in the shadows behind him, heard too late the swish of cloth, and was stayed by a firm hand on his shoulder.

'Well my young rapscallion, and what brings you into my church this Saturday evening? Have you come to pray?'

He saw frank curiosity in the man's eyes, noted the edge of laughter in his voice, and was not afraid.

'No matter. Your arrival is most opportune. My lad is laid up with a fever, and there are services tomorrow. Like to earn yourself some pennies, eh?'

More pennies? His tongue unlocked itself with alacrity.

'Yes please, sir.'

The man's black robes brushed against his bare arm like the feathers of some giant bird as he propelled him gently towards the rear of the church.

'What do they call you, then?' The bird's voice was kind, melodious.

'John Sebastian, sir.'

'A big name for a little fellow. Well, John Sebastian, do you know anything about organs?'

'No, sir.'

'No matter. I shall teach you. It is quite simple.'

The man led the way to some narrow stone steps which twisted up to a gallery. He followed, wondering how he was to earn his pennies. The man emerged, breathing heavily, from the shadows, and something stopped clattering.

In the middle of the gallery was a large wooden contraption reaching from floor almost to the roof. Square wooden towers protruded from it in ascending order of size. In front was a bench before two rows of keys, like a sort of double piano. On either side, were slanting rows of ivory bulbs which, he learned, could be pulled out an inch or two.

'See? These are the stops,' explained the man, demonstrating. He ran his long fingers over the keys and there was the soft cooing as of wood pigeons. He changed the stops, and the pigeons became cuckoos; changed them again and the woodland was transformed into an army marching, then into a street band playing, a drum pounding, a mouse squeaking.

He was entranced. That one pair of hands could do all that. He wanted to be able to do it more than anything in the world.

'Teach me,' he commanded.

The man laughed. 'All in good time. But first I will show you how to earn those pennies.'

'Teach me. Now.' The man hesitated, but he had stood firm.

'As you wish, young master. Sit on the bench beside me, here. Now, watch my hand, and mark the keys I touch.' He spun out a simple melody.

'Now you copy. That's right. But don't strike the keys. It's not a piano. You need only stroke them. That's better.'

It was the tune the men had sung in the fields which he'd already played on the tin whistle he'd found. But on this instrument, it grew into something majestic. It was not until the man had been persuaded to teach him the left-hand accompaniment, that he agreed to be shown how he was to earn his money on the Sunday.

'See, this is the pump. It pumps air into the pipes, just as you blow air into a tin whistle to play it. You must stand here and push this handle up and down all the time I am at the organ. Be sure the lead hanging on that string stays always between those two notches in the wood. Do you understand?'

Of course he'd understood. Then he'd run as fast as he could, across the fields and so onto the road to town, and home. His mother had scolded him, he remembered, for being so late. But his father, when he returned, had praised him and shown genuine delight at his son's determination to learn the organ. Music had been in his life from the start. He remembered his mother singing lullabies to them when he and his brothers were little and his father practising the violin, which he would play at the court of Eisenach. He'd done so well at the pumping that first Sunday, that the organist had begged him to come every week.

All so long ago. Nearly sixty years of air being converted into music. Dear God, but he barely had enough air now for his lungs. And his manuscript so full of corrections because the lamp never seemed bright enough. Composing those forty-eight preludes and fugues as a single piece had taken its toll. But there was still so much to do. He must, he would be well, soon. There was the Mass in B Minor to complete.

As he drifted into dreams, he remembered his first Christmas working at the church. So many candles gleaming like animals' eyes through the branches of fir and pine decorating the walls, the cloying incense hanging on the air like morning mist over the valley, the priest's gold-encrusted vestments, the slow and stately processions. He'd been able to see it all from the gallery. But most of all, the music. The choristers' voices weaving in and out of the organ's thunder, the silver threads of its vast tapestry. Beneath the lamp, in front of the altar, a shepherd boy had sung a lullaby, not a soprano but a rich, brown contralto. The soprano choristers had sung in counterpoint from the forest dark at the rear of the church, as they processed slowly towards the light. The organ contributed a haunting solo flute, only gradually weaving in the other woodwinds, their reeds thin on the cold night air. The strings brought warmth, and the brass strength plus an unexpected tenderness. Smells, sights, sounds, sheer perfection for the senses. He had never forgotten it. Indeed, much of what he heard and felt that night surfaced into his Christmas Oratorio, which moved him as much now as when he wrote it.

By the next Christmas everything had changed.

His father died and his mother married again. At ten, he'd left her and gone to live with his elder brother Christoph, who had recently been appointed assistant organist at a church in Leipzig. It was Christoph who gave him his first proper lessons. He learned fast, was soon playing for services. And so his real life began. Playing the organ, singing as a chorister at Court, learning the viola and violin, composing for them and for the clavichord and organ, and always, before, during and after everything – the teaching. Without teaching, how could he ever have fed his eleven children? Not to mention Anna Magdalena's eight? When all he had ever truly wanted was 'to do some service for God with quiet music whereby to support himself and his family.'

How tired he felt. He would sleep now, just a little. What was it his brothers used to call him when they teased him? Some nickname. John the Pump, was that it? Well, he still had a lot more pumping to do. He'd show them yet.

****

THINK RAINBOW

That evening Robert telephoned, ‘About Wales?’

‘Yes?’

‘Don’t you think it would be better if you came with me, by car?’

Better for whom, thought Susan, but she said, ‘What about Gemma?’

‘She’s not invited. Anyway, she needs to rest. The baby’s due in seven weeks.’

Why must he keep reminding her about the baby? ‘I was going by train,’ she protested, regretting, even as she heard herself say it, the past tense.

‘Don’t be silly. You can’t possibly carry suitcases. I’ll pick you up first thing Friday morning.’

She’d given in to him, as always. Twenty-odd years of being looked after by Robert seemed a hard habit to break. Even now he’d moved in with Gemma who was half his age.

They set off early to avoid the worst of the traffic. Susan knew that, for all his years of driving, Robert was nervous on motorways. She wished he would admit it instead of putting on that guise of bad temper. A little red van shot past them with never a backward glance, to nick itself neatly into the stream of traffic.

'Stupid bastard,' growled Robert, braking suddenly.

Oh God, she thought, it's starting already.

'You feeling all right?'

'Yes, thank you.'

'Got your pills?'

'Yes,' she replied, impatience penetrating her attempts to conceal it. Must he treat her as if she were his aged mother? She'd only had a mild heart attack. It didn't mean she was a total invalid.

They hadn't been long on the motorway before the elements began to work against them. The skies closed in, dark and thunderous.

'I think it's going to rain,' Susan intoned, with a wry sideways look at her husband.

'Bloody forecast wrong again.'

Soon it was raining hard, slashing down diagonally. Over to their left, Birmingham was flooded with sunlight where the sky had torn apart. Oncoming headlamps dazzled, and an errant sunbeam catching at the waves from puddles, created tiny, momentary rainbows beside each car. Susan was entranced. She touched his arm, pointing.

'What?' he barked. His hands looked as if they were glued to the steering wheel.

'Nothing,' she sighed.

Then the rainbow came. It was a full one and hung, glowing, against a black curtain of cloud. She recalled the stories her mother used to tell her when she was little. Of the crock of gold at the end of a rainbow, and of children running through its shining arch to happier lands beyond. She remembered her mother's dark brown voice telling her, when times were bad, to 'Think rainbow, darling.' Perhaps this was a good omen. Would things be different in Wales? She wondered how much the others knew. She'd felt unable to confide in anyone. Not even Jenny, who, of them all, had visited her in the hospital.

'Rob?'

'What?'

'Do Trevor and Cliff know about ... about us?' If he'd told his mates, then the girls would know too.

'No.' The sound came from behind his teeth.

'So, what do you want then? Do we pretend we're still together?'

'We're still married, aren't we?' His tone was one of petulant anger, as if she were winning some argument, and unfairly. Susan was puzzled. She wasn't arguing. 'Anyway, I'm still fond of you, you know that.'

But his voice was not remotely tender. It's just a move in his game, she told herself, and you can be fond of a pet dog. It doesn't mean anything. She turned to look out of the window. It was going to be impossible to fool the girls. They knew her too well.

She must have dozed, for the noisy motorway had gone. They were on a narrow road winding between wooded hills. She could hear water tumbling, and in front of them blue mountains loomed. A strange sense of calm swept over her, almost as if she were coming home. Yet Wales was new to her. It had been Trevor and Mandy's idea to rent a house here for this year's reunion. There would be six, maybe eight, of them this time. They had met up every fifth summer since college. This would be their fourth reunion.

The mountains began to close in, shutting out the green, blocking the sunlight. Isolated sheep stood on the steep, heather-clad slopes, like haricot beans stuck on a collage. Trees gave way to scrub and hawthorn, bowed and beaten. Then came salt and the scent of moon daisies on the air, and at last the sea, glimmering, inviting, impossibly blue.

The house stood alone at the end of a long line of bungalows. It was built of stone with a grey slate roof and looked as if it had always been there. Moss and lichen covered the garden wall, and its many windows were small, like thoughtful eyes.

The front door was flung open and Jenny rushed towards them. She hugged Susan joyfully.

'Isn't it just wonderful here? We're going to have a fabulous time together.' She put one hand up beside her mouth. 'Doug's brought a most peculiar woman. She's called Jo-Hannah, and she has mauve hair.' she giggled.

Susan was relieved to find that she and Robert had been allotted single rooms for she would have found sharing intolerable. Descending in the night for a cup of water, she overheard the other girls discussing her.

'Heart trouble's scary.'

'It's largely Robert's fault, anyway.'

'You mean him going off with that young girl?'

'Got her pregnant, didn't he? No problem. Poor Sue.'

'How do you know?'

'My daughter, Polly, was at Art school with Gemma when she dropped out.'

‘No wonder she looks so down. No kids, no job, no more sports, and no more husband.’

So they had known all the time. Her one consolation was that Robert’s subterfuge had been a waste of effort. As the days passed, she grew sensitive to their cosseting, to the hastily concealed concern. When the others went cycling, she strolled over the bridge to Barmouth. When they climbed Cader Idris, she borrowed Mandy’s watercolours and sketched the estuary. But it was all, for her, mere displacement. So that she didn’t have to think about the future. When she did, alone in the narrow bed, it was as dark as the night.

She spent hours trying to capture the fleeting light on the estuary, the criss-crossing currents when the tide flowed in, the changing colours. But all the time, she was aware of sitting on a time bomb, on a spring held tight by her will alone. A mile of ochre sand, hard and wet, gleamed before her, luring her. The strong muscles of her legs ached to stretch and carry her across that golden strand. If only, all those years ago, it had been the gold. To win a silver medal was great, but oh, how she’d wanted the gold.

‘I like the way you’ve made the sandbanks stand out.’

Susan whipped round. She had not heard him approach. He was old, stooped, dressed in black. He had wispy grey hair and a beard and his skin was yellowish. His eyes were blue and kind and centred on the painting, not her.

‘You’ve a light touch. Have you been painting long?’

‘No. but I’ve always wanted to.’ She wondered who he was. Certainly no holidaymaker.

'Rodrig Owen at your service. I have a house here.' He pointed to the stone house. 'But it's let out at the moment.'

'That's where we're staying.'

'So it is.' He was laughing at her.

The next few days it rained, but their last day dawned bright and fair. Susan, unable to sleep, was up and out before six. She trotted along the sea wall towards the promontory. Two herring gulls were squawking over a piece of fish, and down at the water's edge, she glimpsed the crow-backed figure of Rodrig Owen with his little dog. A brisk wind from the west was gathering fresh storm clouds. It would rain again soon and as quickly be fine again. She stooped to pick up a white pebble. It was round and smooth and nestled in her palm like a talisman. So perfect, so beautiful, this place. And she had been so happy here, these past nine days. She didn't want to leave. She could not bear to think of returning to Ilford with its bittersweet memories, to that dismal street of postage-stamp gardens all snipped and hoovered. There was no life for her there, nor anywhere it seemed.

To her right, heavy clouds were drifting in from Ireland. The first specks of rain fell just as the sun rose above Cader Idris. And there it was again. The rainbow. Scrolling down, soft as chiffon, delicate as watercolour, its seven veils framing a doorway to another world. Clambering down to the hard sand and turning her face to the north, she set her sights on Mawddach Bay, and began to run.

The sheer joy of it. The power flowing through her limbs, its ease and triumph. She was a tiger, a fox before the hounds, she was fleet as a March wind, she was flying.

Leaning into the last curve, the roaring of the crowd in her ears and salt in her mouth, she raced towards the finishing line, the sea, and the rainbow.

The pain kicked in suddenly, ravelling down her arm, screwing heart and lungs into a knot of terror. A choking scream and she was down, her cheek on the wet sand. Her whole world was pain. Then, a strange bitterness beneath her tongue, and, very slowly, the vice on her ribcage eased. The warm body of a dog was wedging itself against her and a grey beard brushed her chin. She looked up in time to see the old man replace a silver pillbox in his waistcoat pocket.

'The rainbow ...' she began.

'Merely transient phenomena.' He regarded her shrewdly. 'One door only leads to another, you know.'

'I didn't want to leave...'

'Then don't. Stay on in my house for as long as you need. Be a housekeeper. My room at the pub suits me well enough.'

He helped her to her feet.

'Remember,' he said, as the sun slanted down on them between puffball clouds, 'it's the journey that matters. No more escape routes. You must live your journey to its natural end.'

His blue eyes in their dark pouches shone. 'And be joyful.'

****

WORDS OF A STRANGER

In the weeks and months which followed, Frank gradually got himself organised. He learned again to cook and remembered to do a weekly wash and to iron his shirts. For something to do and to get himself out of the silent house, he began visiting a union club down on the seafront. He'd come across his old membership card at the back of a drawer. It wasn't really the sort of place he and Rene would have gone to, but it was warm and had a good supply of books and newspapers and he could get a cheese sandwich at the bar.

He found that being out of the bungalow seemed to help distance him from the twilight place he inhabited these days. He felt somehow stuck between her darkness and his own approaching one. Seventy-five, how much longer would he have? He didn't like to think too much about that. These days, he seemed to be waiting rather than living. This time last year, they'd waited for her diagnosis, then for her operation and finally for her place in the hospice. Now he waited for the alarm clock to sound each morning, for the kettle to boil, then for the bus to town, to take him away from the silence.

He'd begun to carry that silence with him, everywhere. Along with darkness. It was like a blanket hanging over him, a blanket cloud. The weather wasn't helping either. November, cold and damp. He couldn't remember when the sun shone last. People's faces too, seemed devoid of smiles. No one spoke to him at the club. Rene had always seemed to find it easy to strike up conversation but Frank didn't know how to start. On bad days, like today, he remembered how she, the more religious one, would say things like 'there'll be a sign, love. You just have to wait'. Waiting again, he thought.

To-day, he'd dozed too long after his beer and sandwich at the club, so had to rush to catch the 4.10 bus home. Due to yet more road works, the bus-stop had been moved fifty yards up the street. He didn't walk so fast these days. They'd sold the car to help pay for a last cruise together.

It was still raining. Water gushed along gutters like mountain torrents, immersing kerb stones, racing down to the ever-waiting sea. And there was scaffolding with vast sheets of plastic flapping, smacking rainwater onto passers-by. So many roads up. It was the same all over town, as if the whole place were being disassembled. Regeneration they called it, but Frank had liked the town as it was. So had Rene. He could barely hear himself think with cars and buses shunting and coughing and grumbling at red lights, diversions, narrow lanes. Then, with a clear run before them, they'd accelerate dangerously, wheels swishing on the steaming roads.

His bus was late. The wind was rising and the tide full up. Still the rain sluiced down. He was cold. He thrust his hands into his pockets. Water dripped from his cap onto his nose. The continuous swish-swash of wet wheels almost drowned out the crashing of waves behind him.

At last his bus came, squelching to a standstill and spurting brown water over his trousers. He pushed his way to the only spare seat. When he glanced at the woman beside him, his heart lurched for she was the image of Rene ten years ago. The same clear skin, soft curls with blond amongst the grey. But her eyes, when she turned to face him, were brown, not blue.

'Will it ever stop raining?' she said.

'We'll need boats soon if it doesn't.' Frank surprised himself by speaking his thought out loud.

'Like Noah's ark?'

Two by two, he thought but did not say.

She rubbed at the steamed-up window with her sleeve. 'Just look at those clouds!'

Huge and heavy and black they rolled in from France. To Frank, they represented his current life, nothing but memories and sorrow. Where was light for him? Where was promise? Then a long orange spear of light slashed the horizon free from the cloud bank. From a reddish gold crevasse, the sunlight came bouncing over the grey sea towards them.

'The sun is still with us after all,' murmured Frank, half to himself.

'Oh, never doubt it,' her smiling eyes reassured him. 'It's only been hiding for a while.'

Could that be it? thought Frank. Was this a sign? A sign that, like the sun, good times would come again? He looked once more at the shining isthmus dividing dark from dark and his heart rose. Life goes on. Perhaps there would still be days of sunshine and laughter. Could this stranger be right? Were they, like the sun, only hiding? He decided to believe her. Anything was better than darkness.

He summoned up a smile as he turned to face her. 'Thank you,' he said. 'Thank you.'

****

OUT OF TOUCH

Her bony fingers plucked insistently at the green coverlet, her many rings gossiping to each other in subdued metallic tones. It was quiet on the ward after lunch, most of us snoozing a bit. I was in for another scrape, a D&C. Barbaric procedure. I was Clare and she a Dorothy nearing the end of her yellow brick road. Forty years separated us.

The staff were jolly with her, encouraging her to eat.

'Come along Dorothy, it's shepherd's pie. Your favourite.'

Personally, I can't imagine that being anyone's favourite. Certainly not Dorothy's. She was too sophisticated by half. And a real Joanna Lumley voice. Every syllable carrying clear across the room.

She only ever had the one visitor, which was one more than I had. He was tall and moved like a big cat. Very aware. Observing him was both restful and disturbing, like coming upon a leopard dozing in the sun. He was soft-spoken with an upper-class accent like hers. Each time, the same grey suit and blue tie, and black briefcase placed carefully on the floor beside his chair. What surprised me was that he never touched her. Never held her hand. Only the last time.

'Stay with me, Gerald. Please.'

'Dear Dorothy. Whatever you ask. As always.'

So not her son, then. I lay there, on the touchline again, observing not participating. All those Saturday matches, cheering on Bill and his team. What a waste of time. Then my blood began to flow, warm, like wetting the bed when you're a child. I knew I should call a nurse but was being lazy about it.

Through the fuzz of my eyelashes, I saw her fingers scurrying and scratching over the sheet like frantic mice, and then his big hands enclosing them, holding them safe so they need not worry any more. And in a little while she was still. Then they came and drew her curtains round.

A nurse with firm, capable hands arrived to mop me up. A bowl of warm water, Imperial Leather soap, soft flannel and fleecy white towel. And Johnson's baby talc for the stubble. She left me feeling blessed and infinitely clean. I was discharged the following day, sent home with a bundle of outsize pads and some little white pills. She warned me that the pills would not prevent conception were I daft enough to risk it. Fat chance.

First thing: I changed my GP. The new one, a Dr. Meakin, offered a brilliant cure for my monthly problem.

'Have another baby,' he suggested blithely.

'At my age?' I responded without thinking. Without bothering to explain to this moronic medic that, failing immaculate conception, I'd need a man.

'Ah yes, of course,' glancing at my notes,' you're much older than you look.'

'Thank … you.' I was only forty-six, for god's sake.

His hands were cold and as insensitive as the rest of him. He poked at me. I silently cursed him with chilblains for all his winters.

Second thing: I put the Maidstone house on the market. Rang Sally to tell her.

'Where am I going to live when I come home?'

'Are you coming home?'

'I might. Anyway, it's Dad's house.'

'No, it isn't. Grandfather left it to me.'

'Oh.'

'What's it like in Santa Lucia?'

'All right. What about my stuff?'

'It can come with me. For now.'

Two years ago, my daughter set off round the world. Got off in South America and has been there ever since. I hope that, whoever he is, he is kind to her.

Steve's response was typical.

'Good for you, Mum. By the way, can you lend me a few quid to tide me over?'

'Over what? Oh, never mind.'

I sent him a hundred. University hasn't changed him. I sold the house to an American family. Cash buyers. All done in a few weeks. Moved into this flat. Nice to be near the sea again. No garden, but a wide balcony overlooking the park.

Third thing: a more congenial job. Settled for receptionist in a solicitor's office. One floor up, double-glazing and a thickish carpet. And my own little cubicle off the waiting-room. Interesting place. Mr. Johns, Mr. Jones and Mr. Jenkins. The three jays.

Mr. Johns wafted in and out like a leaf on a breeze, inconsequential words drifting back from just beyond the swing of a door. Face to face was not his style. If forced into it, his long pale fingers would fumble nervously with his tie as if he'd been caught out in some misdemeanour.

Mr. Jones moved like a bullet. He had unusually long thumbs which were turning into question marks from his habit of hooking them into his waistcoat. He spent most days in Court. Litigation was his life blood.

Mr. Jenkins was older and kind and invariably hunting for his spectacles or their case, a file, or his favourite pen. He would trot in and out of rooms regardless of who was in them, muttering apologetically, until he located the lost item or until he gave up. At which point he would come and chat with me. We'd sit in the sun watching people in the street below. We talked about anything and everything. He was sixty-ish and utterly unshockable. His hands reminded me of my father's. Even the same fine, blond tufts on the backs of his fingers. I knew that if I touched them they'd be as soft as silk. He kept his nails beautifully manicured. Whenever he wrote, he held his pen as if he were drawing, his forefinger straightened out along it.

Fourth thing: I signed up for an evening class. Sculpture for beginners. Be nice, I reckoned, to mould features with my own hands. The clay felt slimy and was, at first, implacably cold and unyielding. But it warmed with kneading, soon becoming pliable under my touch. We were each given a ball of clay to fashion, over the weeks, into a head. I worked to a photo of Sally when she was five. The result was so awful that halfway through term I changed to a shot of my ex-husband. I wouldn't mind if I made a mess of him.

Rory, the teacher, a Dubliner with velvet voice and ragged hair, said it was honest and uncomplicated and could he have it for the end-of-term show? But I had other plans for it. Plans involving a blunt instrument. I felt a lot better afterwards and used the remains in the bottom of flowerpots for drainage. Fitting somehow.

In the second term, I sculpted hands, working from the famous Albrecht Durer print. The clay would not obey me. Those slender, elegant digits persistently eluded me.

'Hands fit for a gorilla,' teased Rory. I felt humiliated. The more so because I half fancied him. I'd even begun to fantasize about those purposeful fingers stroking my shoulders, my neck, my throat. First time such dreams had visited since the imprint of a fist was left on my cheek.

Even in our early days, Bill had been a clumsy and infrequent lover. He used to grab hold of me as if he were playing rugger.

I tore up Durer, ascribed the jumbo fists to a non-existent farmer uncle and put them in the next show. Mr. Jenkins came to view our little exhibition, seeming interested but not saying much. He invited me to dinner.

'My wife and I are having a few friends round. Give you a chance to meet people.'

He was right, I knew. Apart from the sculpture class and work, I never went out. This was partly due to my continuing anatomical problems. Reluctantly, I returned to my old GP., who referred me back to the hospital. Supervised by the consultant, an absurdly young student doctor examined me. He probed where only a lover should go, his gloved hands nuzzling tentatively like some shy woodland creature.

The consultant was impatient. 'Don't hang about. No lady wants you in there any longer than is strictly necessary.'

The poor guy blushed, withdrawing his hand so roughly that my body instinctively responded. It's debatable which of us was the more embarrassed.

The consultant's investigation was swift and expert.

'You've rather a large fibroid. I'll put you on my hysterectomy waiting list.'

The thought of getting rid of it all, for ever. Yes, oh yes!

Exhibition over, I brought my hands home. Put them on a table by the window. Then by my bed. Just before dropping off to sleep, I'd fondle them, enjoying their hills and valleys, the smooth cone of each rounded knuckle, the set of each wrist, the thin curve of the nails. Had I made the nails a bit too long? For what? What was I thinking about? In my dreams, those hands of clay grew soft and tender as they lay alongside a thigh or heavy on my stomach or couching a breast.

It was the day before the Jenkins' dinner party. So, fifth thing: a new dress. Something black and clingy. Not too short as thighs not my best asset. And a stole maybe. Found a 1920's shawl thing in black lace. Sexy. Had my hair fixed with a false chignon. Treated myself to a manicure.

Mr. J's house was smaller than I'd imagined. More ordinary, and his wife homely and very Welsh. She emerged from the kitchen, plump hands all floury.

'Davy's told me so much about you. And what a lovely dress. I'd better not shake hands though …' and she flicked powdery fingers at an errant curl.

The food smelled delicious, so I said so.

The lounge was filled with roses. Bowls of them everywhere. Gentle lighting. I ran my finger down the full-length curtains of azure and bronze. They were stiff like taffeta. The corner sofa was cream and of the softest leather.

Other guests began to arrive. Tom, with emery-board hands, the skin taut as if it had shrunk. His wife, Alice, the merest brush of fingertips, but sharp-edged. A small, dark man called Ernest, with damp and gummy paws (second hand over mine). Annabel. All red, black and silver, scarlet talons clutching at my shoulders and a glancing, perfumed kiss.

Then, from the hall, a voice I knew. Soft-spoken, upper-class. My palms itched. Still a grey suit but silk this time, and a different tie. His huge, steady hands embraced mine. His eyes were grey-green and slightly questioning.

'Have we met before?'

'I don't think so.'

How could he possibly have noticed me, flat on my back, on the opposite side of the ward?

Mr. J. trotted in, a fleck of dough on his lapel.

'Gerald is a barrister.' His tone revealed personal pride. 'As well as being my kid brother.' He patted his arm affectionately.

So. Gerald Jenkins. Hmm. Clare Jenkins? Better. He escorted me to the dining-room. My head was level with his shoulder. We had soup, I think, and Welsh beef. Though I do remember the syllabub, thistledown on the tongue. But I was busy learning his hands. The skin a manilla shade, the pattern of the bones not obscured by surplus flesh, a satiny gleam of soft down, smooth nails, their half-moons clear. All the joints looked supple, indicating activity. I wondered what he did, apart from law.

That such large hands could be so sensitive to the slightest reflex. No more explanation, I was in touch again. It was midnight when we realised all the others had gone. Gerald was telling me about Dorothy.

'She was my very first client. Acted with Sir Laurence Olivier once, you know. Lovely lady. I would have done anything for her.'

Mrs. Jenkins entered with a tray. Our coffees had long since gone cold. She noted our threaded fingers and smiled gently.

****

AN AFTERNOON IN THE PARK

'It all began in a park like this.' With one wave she encompasses four hectares.

'No. We met in the church hall. It rained so the fete was held indoors. You remember?'

'Yes. I remember how I felt you staring at me. Then, when I turned my head, you looked away.'

'I was afraid you'd see.' He is not looking at her.

'I did see.'

'I wanted you … to see. Then you walked right up to me and touched my arm.'

'I asked you a question.' She looks away to her right, where ducks bask on the grassy bank.

'Yes, you came straight up to me and asked me who I was. I could hardly believe my luck.'

'You bought two mugs of tea and we sat at a plastic table. You kept spooning sugar into yours. It must have been thick with it.'

'I couldn't take my eyes off you. We talked for nearly an hour. That's when it all began.'

'No Pierre, it began in the park.'

'I never went into parks. There wasn't time.'

She continues glancing about her as she speaks. He gazes steadily at his feet.

'There's something attractive about a park, don't you think? Nature within boundaries. Trees and flowers confined to their appointed places. No passionate rampaging. Like that forsythia over there, safely staked and tied.'

'So, in exchange for protection, their activities are limited?' He ignores her pointing finger.

'I guess so. A bit like you and me, eh?'

He laughs ruefully, a soft growl in his grey beard. In front of them, the sun dances in golden daggers on the lake's surface. The afternoon is honeysuckle heavy, not a breath of wind. He is hot in his shirtsleeves, she perspiring beneath a floral blouse. Where silver birches rustle, a narrow path turns like a bent finger, beckoning. He can smell violets, suspects a flowerbed nearby. Hidden, a blackbird is singing.

'I met my first boyfriend in a park, a dusty London park. He courted me shyly in spring, more boldly in summer greens. But when dank autumn overtook us and the affair was translated to a backstreet bed-sit, the whole thing seemed too tawdry for words.'

'Let's stroll a little, shall we? Find a seat in the shade. If there is one.'

They rise, he more slowly, not using his stick which is still folded up. She puts out an arm to support him, then thinks better of it. Together, yet not quite together, they amble round the water's edge. On a farther shore where it is shallow and there is a patch of imported sand, children paddle and a dog splashes in and out. Their distant shrieks and his excited barking are the only sounds to be heard.

'There is shade here.' He pauses beside a bench but she hesitates, noticing that bushes hang too low over it.

'Too much. Dapple shade is better. Let's try the next one.'

They pass where the twisty path beckons the unwary into deep woods. He does not see it, but she shivers without knowing why. At the next seat, they resettle themselves, she to his left this time. This used to be her preferred place when with him because he had once said her right profile was the more beautiful. They are silent, each lost in a drift of memories.

'A park is such a magical place.'

'I imagine it could also harbour dangers.'

'Ah, but if things get out of hand, you make for the nearest exit. A clanging gate gives the no-go sign as clearly to an aggressive dog as to a clumsy pick-up.'

He ponders this but asks anyway.

' When did you see me in a park, then?'

'I didn't.'

'But you said …'

'No, Pierre, I saw you from the park.'

'Tell me. Again.'

He relaxes, stretching out his long legs, half-wondering why he can still smell violets.

'One day last summer …'

'Only one year ago?'

'… well, we can pretend, can't we?'

She laughs, puts her hand into his where it rests on his thigh. He dare not respond. After a few moments, she withdraws it.

'I was staying at Sally's and took a short cut through the park. I was pretty low at the time. Sort of lost.'

'Had you lost someone?'

'No, just had a surfeit of reality. Which was possibly why the park attracted me.'

'I don't understand.'

'A park's a pretend world, where everything's kept neat and nice. Where grown-ups as well as children play under the illusion that the big wide world beyond will not intrude. And when the sun goes down and the park-keeper rattles his keys, the games are over. Then we all say goodbye and go home to tea.'

'What happened there?'

'Everything changed. I changed.'

'How did you change?'

'First I saw myself in the lake. Then I saw you.'

'My reflection in the lake?'

'No. Not there. Later.'

'Where then?'

'I'd entered by the archway, do you remember it? It was my first visit and I wasn't sure which path to follow. I sort of trusted the park to guide me.'

She half-laughs as if remembering the romantic girl she once was. He remembers her too. And the tale she is telling. How good to hear her voice again. The way she meanders through her tale still both entrances and irritates him.

'It rained, short and sharp, I remember, drenching me. My hair clung to my neck. The paths were slate shiny and trees dripped on me. I saw a blackbird balancing on a cable singing his heart out. His feathers gleamed like cannel coal. Steam rose from lawns as if there were geysers beneath them. My path divided. To the right it ran straight to a boundary gate. The left led a rolling way down to a stream and a humpy little bridge.'

'Which did you choose?'

'The left, of course.'

'The sinister one?'

'Yes, it pulled at me.'

'No evil can follow you across water.'

'I watched the stream dashing along, smoothing stones and washing away debris from crevices. I thought of baptism, of purifying water, of how it spawns new life, and all the knots of anger and resentment began to uncoil, their long filaments slipping away downstream. Let it all go, I thought. Bitter-sweet boyfriend years, pointless skirmishes, the boredom of my job ...'

'You let it all go?'

She sighs long and deep at her memory of the moment, her whole body easing.

'Ye-e-e-s.' She breathes the word. 'And there you were.'

'What? Where was I?' He has forgotten this part.

'Standing on a little hill above the stream. Still as a rock you were. On the other side of the fence.'

'In the real world?'

'Yes. That's how I knew.'

'Knew what?'

'That it wouldn't be a game. That, with you, it would be real.'

'I don't play games.'

'No, you never have. Thank God.'

He strives to recall why he might have been standing and staring into a park. He was not a contemplative in those days. Life had been full of action. He gives up. Too long ago. But there's still one thing.

'How did you know?'

'What?'

'That we were going to … I mean, you couldn't have known. Could you?'

'Dear man, I honestly don't understand it, even now. But the second I saw you waiting there, it was as if an invisible line already joined us. When you walked away, I felt it tug.'

'So how did you find me?' He's annoyed he can't recall this bit.

'It was Sally. She dragged me along to help her on the baby clothes stall. She knitted them all herself.'

'Do you knit?'

'You know I can't! I began that green pullover for you the month we met and it was still unfinished when we parted. How many years was that?'

He doesn't want to remember, doesn't want to wrap up their time together into a neat parcel labelled three or five or however many years it was. He'd never wanted their time to have an ending. It had been forced upon them. It hurts him to recall even the edge of the pain he suffered. How she must have suffered, he cannot bear to imagine. He sees she has moved on, but his pain resides still in his heart, its claws dug deep. This accidental meeting, lovely though it has been, he would rather have avoided. He will not come here again.

The afternoon heat is fading, sunshine filtering through trees now and a breeze scurrying little waves across the surface of the lake. The children have all gone home.

'What time is it?'

His abrupt question surprises her. She checks her wristwatch.

'Nearly four. Why?'

'I must go soon. You must go too, Anna.'

It is the first time he has used her name since they, quite literally, bumped into each other on the path to the lake. Glancing across the water, she spies a small, dumpy figure marching in their direction.

'Pierre …'

'Go, Anna. Please.' His voice is hard, verging on cold.

'Pierre … all right, I'm going, but … just look at me, will you? One last time? You haven't looked at me properly all afternoon.'

How much he longs to gaze on her beloved face, she will never know.

'Anna …' He is half-turning as she bends to retrieve her bag. But his acute hearing judges those determined feet to be no more than twenty-five yards away.

'Please go. Now.'

He hears her sharp indrawn breath.

'Dear God! It's Beth! I thought your wife had …'

'I beg you.'

She goes, swiftly. His ears follow her receding steps, knows she has turned into the woods, guesses she has done this to be out of sight quickly, and breathes a sigh of relief. The generous body of his wife plumps down beside him.

'Well, I must say, it's really lovely here. Well worth the drive. This lake's twice the size of the one in our park. I expect there's a cafe somewhere. Shall we go and find it? A cup of tea and a gooey cake, you'd like that, Pierre, wouldn't you?'

He is used to being offered that which she knows he does not want and which they both know she wants for herself. Mostly he gives in for the sake of peace. But not today.

'Can we go home? I'm so tired.'

'Did you walk too far again? You know what the doctor said. But you always think you know best, don't you?'

He sees no point in answering.

'Who was that woman?'

'Which woman?'

'The one leaning all over you. I saw her. Scuttled off when she saw me coming, didn't she? Couldn't even wait to say hello.'

'Had to get back to her husband.'

He realises the second he has spoken that it would have been wiser to keep quiet.

'You do know her? Who is she? Where did we meet her? Did you know she was coming here today?'

'I didn't know I was coming here today. I'm not even sure where here is.'

'What were you talking about?'

'Eh?'

'You and that woman? I know I've seen her before somewhere. I wish I could remember.'

He prays silently that she will not.

'We just passed the time of day,' he soothes. 'Parks are only pretend worlds, nothing's real here. Strangers meet, exchange platitudes and pass on. It's what parks are for.'

'You want me to bring you here again next week, then?'

'No. I think our little park is far nicer. And I can wait for you in the teashop there.'

Her wristwatch beeps.

'Goodness! Is that the time?'

She leaps up, hooks her arm in his and hauls him to his feet. 'I don't want to hit the rush-hour.'

His stick, still folded, clatters to the ground. She scoops it up, shaking it out to its full-length, and shoving it into his hand.

'What's the use of me buying you a white stick if you're ashamed to use it?'

'I don't need it here, in a park.'

'Oh, of course, a park, according to you, is a pretend place. And what if you fell in the lake? That'd be real enough!'

She rattles on, all the way home. He does not listen. He stopped listening to her years ago. He can still feel the soft touch of Anna's hand in his. Later, while his wife fusses in the kitchen and he is at last alone, he buries his nose, his lips into the palm of his hand, breathing in once again the sweet scent of her hand.

****

MAP-READING

With her delicate forefinger she is tracing his lines, blue wiggly lines like rivers meandering, lowland veins ferrying his lifeblood. Crossing them are darker lines; she imagines Irish navvies slaving, iron horses steaming between startled fields. Scarlet lines weave magic into themselves like old roads linking towns, villages, lovers. Here and there, a scar, almost straight, like a mad motorway roaring from city to crazy city.

He stretches out, yawns contentedly. The Persian cat on the window sill echoes his movements.

Eyes closed, she murmurs names, probing ever northward. She began with the toe of Cornwall, now the rivers Tamar, Dart and Exe, still waters running deep, meeting salt on flood tides. Then Exmoor's hidden valleys, red fox running, and the green of the Somerset Levels. Already she's brushing the shank of the Cotswolds, little finger teasing the Severn estuary. Thence to Birmingham, middle finger pressing hard on its darkened navel.

Languidly, he turns over, spread-eagled on the duvet. The bed creaks.

She reaches Liverpool, ring finger stroking the Mersey, then drags her thumbnail up the spine of the Pennines. He grunts. At Windermere she kisses each lake, remembering. She plunges her whole hand into the Solway Firth, and she's over the border. Touching Glasgow and Edinburgh, she uses both hands.

He rolls onto his back again. 'You've a good memory,' he says, smiling lazily.

Her index finger pinpoints Perth, Dundee, the silver Tay.

'What about the western isles?' he says.

She shifts, left hand over Argyle, caresses Mull and Skye, and the Lewis.

'The tangle of the Isles,' she croons.

'With heather honey taste upon each name,' he sings, to the same tune.

She changes tack. Her left hand grazes Ullapool, the blunt blade of Suilven, points to Forsinard.

'You've missed out Tongue and the northern coast,' he says.

She laughs as they put it right.

'You've a good memory,' he says again, his hand on her back. 'Land's End to John O'Groats. All the way.'

'Yes,' she says, 'all roads lead to this. Don't they?'

'I guess they do,' he says, pulling her down onto him and kissing her fingers one by one.

****

LIFE CHANGES

This must be how flying felt. The moment of a bird's take-off. These new Nikes were really something. It was like running on a sea of balloons. Worth every penny. Fortunately, Stefan wouldn't know just how many pennies. Gone to London again, to sort out a visa for his supposed cousin, Sofia.

He and Gina didn't talk much these days. She wasn't sure why. It had been a gradual thing. No arguments, just increasing absence. When she told him about the half-marathon, he'd looked at her as if he no longer knew her, and said, 'Aren't you a bit old for that?', which immediately made her feel she was. But forty-five was nothing. People ran it in their seventies. True, she was no Paula Radcliffe. She was heavier for one thing, as well as being blessedly curvier.

And Tracy, on the ward, the other day, 'What are you running away from?' with that sharp professional look of hers.

But Gina loved running for its own sake. There wasn't any more to it. Was there? This morning was her first time running straight from work. First the flat four miles of The

Ridge, then right, through Ore village – Easter eggs already hanging in the newsagent's window – swinging left at the *Sussex Arms*, and so down the long rolling hill to the sea. She was making good time. But rhythm was important too. And balance.

Along The Bourne, the clatter of a late dray, the syrupy tang of spilt beer mingling uneasily with nostril-coating fishy smells from the strand and warm diesel fumes from an overnight lorry trundling dozily out of the carpark. An acid stab of Jeyes as she passed the public loos. On past the silent slot machines, the boating-lake and crazy golf. Then the pier and the chequered promenade where a shriek of gulls rose overhead, scimitar wings cleaving the pale sky. It was good to be alive. In spite of Stefan and all that.

It was Fran who goaded her into things.

'Time you got a life,' she'd said, 'and stopped relying on that part-time husband of yours.'

'I've got friends at work. And you.'

'That's not enough. You should make some new friends, away from sickness and disease. Join a club, do a course.'

'Is that a dare?'

'No. It's an order.'

No matter how long retired, when a senior nursing officer gives an order, you jump. Gina signed on to a course at the college that very evening. Mythology. Well, it had to be a Thursday and she didn't fancy Russian, bricklaying, or sculpture.

They were a lively group, and this term it was trees. He'd brought in pictures of vast South American forests that you could lose yourself in. Juan de Silvero. She could listen to his voice all day. Its soft tones made her think of deep brown trees, of canopies swaying, of rich green shadows. She'd planted the seeds he gave her, and already their dark, alien leaves were shrouding her rose bed.

She found herself imagining how it would be running alongside him. His loping stride, his languorous yet concentrated movements. Like a big cat. He was both predatory and benevolent. The sheen of his blue-black hair, those amber eyes. Shrewd. Other.

She glanced at her watch. She'd lost her rhythm, let the hill run away with her. Oh well, might as well carry on home. She'd never understood why Stefan bought the house on the Bexhill Road. So noisy, her plants dying and their front door permanently grimy. Though the back was a bonus. She loved to sit at the open bedroom window on these nights without Stefan and listen to foxes barking and feral cats hunting over by Bexhill tip. Six miles of open country before the scattered lights of Crowhurst. Some nights she heard other cries, and once, she glimpsed a strange, sombre shape padding through the long grass just beyond the garden gate.

It was no good. She felt too exhausted to run any further. She would call on Fran, who was another early riser, at Grosvenor Gardens. See how she was keeping. She thumbed the buzzer. She hated entry phones.

'Fran?'

'Gina, my dear. What a lovely surprise. Come on up.'

The door opened as of its own accord, admitting her into its lino-dim hallway. Fran's fuzzy blonde head appeared above the banister, a smiling sunflower in a barren, brown garden.

'My, you do look hot. A drink, perhaps?'

'Just water, thanks.'

But within minutes, Gina found herself perched beside Fran on the window-seat, balancing a cup of tea and eyeing a hastily produced sponge cake with more than passing interest.

Fran, her closest friend, must be seventy now, but was as good a listener as ever. And Gina still got nursing tips from her.

They chatted of this and that. Gina wanted to know about the tests Fran had mentioned last time but was afraid to ask. She observed her friend, noting the thinner arms, the looser neck, those work-worn fingers picking at crumbs on the gold-rimmed plate.

Fran probed with medical precision and Gina knew she could hide nothing from her. Things she'd not admitted to herself even.

'How's the class going?'

'Fine. It's the mythology of trees and forests this term.'

'Ah, the symbols of life and regeneration?'

'Yes, the Tree of Life ...'

'And Eve's apple tree?' interrupted Fran.

'... in the sacred grove. And Proteus again.'

'I thought he was a sea-god?'

'Yes, he is. But if you can catch him when he's asleep under a tree and bind him fast so he cannot change his shape, then he has to tell you your future.'

'I'm not sure I want to know mine.'

She leaned across to refill Gina's cup. The muscles of her upper arm hung, a half-moon pendulum. The teapot grated onto its tile base. A bottle of pills stood on a side table. Pink ones, which Gina recognised.

'And this Juan what's-his-name?'

Gina started and couldn't stop. The pictures, his voice, the stories he told them. Especially those about the jaguar, the king of the forest.

Fran interrupted her in mid-sentence, her blue eyes deepening, her voice almost sharp.

'When?' she said.

And Gina relived it for her. The warm fragrance of his breath when he stood close to her. Like almond blossom. But his gloves, that's when it really began. The pointed shape of them, the imprint of his nails on the soft leather still visible long after he'd laid them on his desk. Their earthy scent when she'd held them to her cheek. She'd returned them, of course, the following Thursday. That was the evening he told them tales of the divine hunt, of the magic power of shamans. And the art of shapeshifting.

Fran's back straightened, the restless fingers stilled themselves.

'Did he mention any particular drug in connection with that?' she enquired and proceeded to reveal a whole chunk of her life that was completely new to Gina.

'My Harry was a doctor, you know. He and I worked in Amazon country for more than fifteen years. The natives used *ayahuasco*, amongst other drugs. I can lend you a book about it if you like.'

She pulled a leather-bound volume from the bookcase. As it left its niche, Gina glimpsed a second bottle of capsules which, with a jolt of fear, she also recognised. Her unvoiced questions were answered. It would seem that Fran had arranged an exit visa for herself should life get too tough, the pain too bad.

As they parted, Fran uncharacteristically hugged her. Gina's practised hands registered the lean frame, the stepped ribs.

'Good luck, Gina.'

'For the half-marathon?'

'What else?'

But her eyes revealed what else. For a second, Gina found herself gazing into a face alight with remembered love. The next moment she could see only a sick, old woman who she loved, with too many shadows on her face.

She returned home to a more than half-expected final e-mail from Stefan. So that was that. She supposed she would be sensible, as he requested, and not think too much about Sofia who was twenty years younger than them both.

She spent much of the day reading Fran's book. Then, in the evening, she took her supper up to the back bedroom and ate it by the open window. Then she lay diagonally across the wide bed, dozing and dreaming, while a cool, partially eclipsed moon regarded her shrewdly. A little before midnight, she descended to the jade shadows of the garden and carefully plucked some of the deep-veined leaves now towering far above her roses. She chopped them, poured boiling water over them and stirred the resulting emerald liquid meditatively. When the concoction was cool enough, she drank it. Her expression was dreamy yet speculative. Then she began to pace the length of the garden with growing excitement.

Soon, above the night rustlings and distant barking of foxes, she discerned a different call. A big cat's cry. Closer. She breathed his name, light as a moth wing on the night air. 'Juan'. Then, beside her, the scent of almonds and a warm, inviting, purring growl which made her think of deep brown trees, of canopies swaying, of rich green shadows.

The garden gate clicked open. And she began to run.

****

AFTER

Sunlight bouncing off car roof is enough to make you blink it streaks from knives and forks into my eyes half-blinds me could have sat down there amongst the old dears the never-have-a-man-again ones the drove-my-husband-to-his-grave ones do women always outlive their menfolk like we were there before they got born and will be long after they're gone like me with Troy before during and – now shall I have the set menu for eleven ninety five or go wildly a la carte something exotic sounding like mullet or monkfish got a face like an ugly old man I hate cutting heads off fish the final betrayal lifting its lid and all the innards coming out on a long red string like an afterbirth death and birth thing again can't I ever see anything else here comes the waitress her face says I'm not a regular here so what am I doing on the favoured table the one on the dais the only one with a decent view hurts my eyes to look at the sea sun so brilliant water glitters word sounds ominous sea of diamonds are dangerous greed glitters – there's Beachy Head seventeen miles away landfall waitress waiting that's a good one wonder how many times she's asked me miles away I was over the sea to – steak and kidney pie ugh the smell of cooking flesh no thank you and it's innards again best be polite just say goodbye and none of all that how could you and why didn't you and if only ….just walk away head up shoulders back bum tight hope I still look good to him hope he calls me back of course he won't dare not wouldn't dare wear skirt as short as that nails too long unhygienic and green like witches eyes to match never had mullet before a tiny risk a step into the – before during and – what did she mean only tomato or carrot soup or juice can't face either why is everything red and runny don't think of it walk away – red fish too can't get away soup or fruit juice, only tomato or carrot what did she mean doesn't matter always trying to define things that don't matter any more like can't see you again can I see you again and your smile when exactly did it begin that first look locking of eyes the picnic or the train before I knew your name even when that accepting glance that certain thing understood did I see and not recognise it surely I would have known did I miss it why torment myself this need to pinpoint the beginning so can draw in its cord to the moment of ending a bag of memories to be put away out of sight under the bed that day your wife got home early feeling randy as randy as we had been only hours before no time no back way out on the seventh floor god but I wanted to laugh with the springs bashing away above my head my place after that never again we said and so never again nevermore nevermore just eat the fish be a good girl don't think about its red skin blushing flushing – how do fish make love no problem sweating cool in the water so many fish all look the same any one will do lots more fish in the sea why's that guy looking at me thought they were all old women is he alone nice hands no paunch eating fish with salad – before during and – plenty more fish in the sea – and after.

****

THE CREATIVE WRITING CLASS

She'd come in off the streets, literally, by the look of her. Greasy old mackintosh which had once been green or brown and which was secured at her waist with a piece of rope, all buttons having long since flown. Her grey hair was matted, the ends wet and windblown for there was a gale that day. Her crepe soles squeaked on the vinyl flooring. She could have been any age from sixty to ninety, but there was something about her, and her blue eyes were bright with curiosity.

Miss Whittle, the teacher, was worried. With all this bad weather, the numbers were dropping. She had to make them up or the class would be closed. And she did so need the money let alone a few precious hours away from her drunken husband. And from Mother. At least her husband slept. So when Aggie peered hopefully round the door, Miss Whittle was inclined to enrol her first and ask questions after. Bums on seats were what she needed. Old Jack, the hall's caretaker, had said he might join too. But then you never knew with caretakers.

Seated in the middle of the front row, Aggie looked around herself with interest.

‘What do you do here?’ she asked her neighbour.

Mrs. Sparrow turned to her, sniffing suspiciously. Something as dirty as that just had to smell.

‘Write stories then read them out.’

‘Oh, I love stories. And poems. Especially ballads.’

Miss Whittle rapped on her desk for attention. The subject that week was ‘Schooldays’ and most had written personal stories. Only one, Miriam, read out a fictional tale. She was surprised and flattered when it was greeted by a burst of delighted clapping from the front row.

‘Oh capital! Capital!’ crowed Aggie, not at all abashed to be the only one to respond so enthusiastically. ‘You tell a good tale, missus. Have you got any more stories like that?’

Without waiting for Miriam’s reply, Aggie announced excitedly to all and sundry that she had a story she could tell them. Miss Whittle, glancing up at the clock, said hurriedly, ‘Not now, Aggie. Perhaps next week?’ The woman unnerved her somehow.

They didn’t really expect to see her again but at the following class, there was Aggie in the front row, a brand new A4 pad on the table in front of her. It was the cleanest thing about her.

Good god! Could she actually write, thought Miss Whittle who had half-expected her merely to make her mark on the enrolment sheet. But Aggie had filled it in neatly and paid the full fee in cash. She noted that her address was a Victorian terrace at the poorer end of town.

This time, the subject set was ‘The Countryside’. Mrs. Sparrow spoke about her childhood in a country parsonage and Roger read a pompous piece on care of the environment. Others had brought verses and one a story written from a badger's point of view. This last held Aggie's attention most. She turned her chair round so she could watch the face of the reader.

'My turn now?' she asked wistfully when it was ended.

'No, it's coffee time,' said Miss Whittle. She'd caught sight of several pages filled with a tiny bird-like script. She really must emphasize the necessity to be brief.

After coffee she gave them a few fun exercises to do. In the pause which followed the last one, Aggie again tried to read her piece but Miss Whittle stopped her gently.

'Not now, Aggie, there isn't enough time.'

And so it went on, week by week. Yet Aggie continued to come, bringing fresh work each time. She listened eagerly to everything and was never slow to show her appreciation.

Eventually, Roger and Miriam and some of the others put pressure on Miss Whittle, saying it just wasn't fair. Miss Whittle relented on the condition it was something really short, a description or a poem.

The ensuing weeks provided the class with the kind of surprised delight Aggie herself had shown at hearing their stories. Against her will, Miss Whittle acknowledged that Aggie definitely had potential as a poet. A bit obscure at times, she thought, and some weird imagery.

Aggie read out poems about badgers and birds and all creatures of the countryside and about urban foxes. Later, when she felt more at ease, there were ballads about her friends and the tales they told each other around their night fires. By Christmas, her words had so charmed them that all but a few no longer paid much attention to her appearance. They were as eager as little children for the next dose of magic.

It was in January that things changed. Aggie missed the first class of term. A grubby little urchin waylaid Miss Whittle as she got out of her car, saying that Aggie was ill in bed and the doctor said she must be careful.

It was during their coffee-break that Mrs. Sparrow flourished a book she had been given as a Christmas present. The title on its dust jacket was clear for all to see. 'Life on Hill and Heath' by Diana Coppard.

'Look!' she said, obviously enjoying herself, 'Read these! You'll soon recognise them. I always knew she was a fraud!'

They crowded round as she turned the pages and there before them, each one delicately illustrated, were the poems Aggie had been reading out to them. But there was no sign of the ballads.

Miss Whittle was surprised at her conflicting reactions. The prim part of her felt justified that a woman who looked like a tramp had been revealed as dishonest and a cheat. It fitted one's preconceptions. Yet another part of her felt compassion. Poor old dear. Did it really matter whose poems they were? Their lives had all been enriched by them. She tried to put this over to the class. Some agreed but it was plain that others felt safer in their condemnation of her.

It was three weeks before Aggie reappeared. Her voice was thick, and she coughed frequently into a voluminous handkerchief. It was obvious she was aware of the hostile atmosphere which greeted her for she sat very quiet during the readings.

Immediately after coffee-time and before Miss Whittle could get going, Mrs. Sparrow took charge.

'Have you got a poem for us, Aggie?' she asked, baiting the trap.

The old woman's eyes lit up and she flicked through the pages of her A4 pad.

'I've got poems, and a story,' she said with pride in her voice, ' a Christmas story.'

This had been the subject set three weeks previously. She had offered them stories before but had never been given a chance to read them.

'We want one of your poems, Aggie,' they chorused, some wanting to catch her out, others to be beguiled yet again by her magical words.

Judge and jury were centred on Mrs. Sparrow who sat ready, with the open book on her lap.

'All right,' said Aggie, and began in a croaky voice, 'Milk white snow carpets a valley, icicles prismatic hang from a barn, out steps a timid fox ...'

A single word cut her short.

'Liar!'

Mrs. Sparrow stood up and thrust the book in front of Aggie, the page open at those very words.

'How dare you! All these poems you've been reading to us, they're all here, in this book. Diana Coppard wrote them. Not Aggie whatever-your-name-is.'

Aggie had also risen to her feet. She looked Mrs. Sparrow straight in the eye.

'Agnes Copple's my name. And I'm Diana Coppard too. That was my pen name.'

'Don't be ridiculous. This book was published in 1947. You can't possibly be that old. This is a new edition. I've rung the publishers and they said Diana Coppard died years ago.'

'Did she? Funny I never heard about it. Funnier still that they've brought out a new edition and not told me. The rotters!'

'If you really are a published poet,' queried Miss Whittle, 'how is it that you're, I mean … .' She tailed off.

'How is it I'm not wearing furs and travelling in my Rolls, you mean?'

'Well, sort of … '

'There's no money in poetry, my girl. You lot should know that. Wrote all those poems in my twenties. Sold well at the time, but it's been out of print for years. Now some bright spark's found it. Should have done his homework though. I suppose I'll have to fight for my royalties. Nothing changes, does it?'

Aggie did not return to the writing class. Once the publishers realised their mistake, they naturally cashed in on her still being alive. They provided her with new clothes and a chauffeur-driven car. She celebrated her ninety-fifth birthday at the Television Centre and signed endless copies of 'Life on Heath and Hill'. The stories she had begun writing only recently were described by reviewers as succinct and witty observations of a group of would-be writers and a collection was published posthumously a year later.

****

SNAKES AND LADDERS

Monday 5th January

Meant to start this on the first ... It's been a snake of a week, as young Robbie would say. Still, better late than never. So here beginneth the diary of Sally Finch, wife - no - widow, and grandmother, aged fifty-one. Just.

Haven't kept a diary since I was at school. Never had time. Not with my job and Alan and the kids. Now there's just me, I've no excuse. Karen says audio diaries are all the rage. Suppose I'll get the hang of it eventually. No hint of her coming home yet. What with her in Australia and Robert in Canada, well, it's at Christmas that you really miss your family, isn't it? I used to have young Robbie here most weekends. Wonder if he misses our games? Beat-Your-Neighbour-Out-of-Doors, Frustration, Snakes and Ladders – that was our favourite.

Rained today. Missed my bus, so walked to work. Gulls' shit on the pavement. Sea and sky the same gun-metal grey. Snow threatening. Not a touch of brightness anywhere.

Dora in and out of Miss Phillips' office. Something going on. Caught Tracey's eye, but she just winked and patted the side of her nose so I'm none the wiser. New chap in the kitchen. A cook, I think, not a porter.

Tuesday 6th January

On lates today. Nearly ten when I got home. Absolutely shattered. Just a minute, I'll turn the telly off. That's better. Well, the mystery's solved. Dora's taking early retirement, leaves at Easter. Tracey, Charlie and me get first refusal of her job. I must say the extra money would be nice. Not to mention the perks.

Letter from Joan. Wants me to sell my mausoleum, as she calls it, and buy a flat near her, up north. I know I don't need this big house anymore, but … What I'd really like is a little café, somewhere warm. Red-checked tablecloths, blue sky, and a blue sea below. Wish I could just roll the dice and shoot up a ladder to a better place. The new cook's Greek or Turkish or something. Quiet. Different. His name's Gaspar, I think.

Wednesday 7th January

My Rest Day. Cleaned the house from top to bottom. Took four bags down to Oxfam. Rob's records and Alan's clothes. Well, it's best part of two years now. Posted reply to Joan. Said I'd think about it. Posted off my application for Dining-Room Supervisor. Can't see Charlie getting it. He doesn't even know the meaning of punctuality. Nor of deodorant. We all have to stand up wind of him. And Tracey's so clumsy. Drops anything that's not stuck to her. Built like a steamroller, she is. Smokes fags that smell like a dung-heap.

Nipped down to the corner-shop this evening, for a quarter bottle of Courvoisier. Helps me sleep. Tall guy meandering in front of me. And it's Gaspar. 'Didn't know you shopped here,' I said. Silly thing to say. He's what Joan would call a fine figure of a man. You feel safer with a big man, somehow.

Thursday 8th January

Dora's Rest Day. Snakes abounding. Tracey already acting like she's in charge. Realise why when this Cher look-alike trips in behind Miss Phillips, clipboard in hand. The outside observer. I go on the till and think, 'That's funny, where's all the change gone?' The nurses stream in, all coffees and Kit-Kats and a string of fivers. The nurses, poor kids, only get fifteen minutes, so I tell 'em to pay later. 'Cher' scribbles furiously, Miss Phillips chews on her Valium and Tracey's looking so smug, I know immediately it was her. 'You just wait,' I hiss. 'I'm sure I don't know what you mean,' she pipes, all injured innocence.

Lunchtime was hell. Ran out of knives. Twice.

Tennis on the telly this evening. That Australian bloke. Big feller, nice thighs, as Karen would say.

Friday 9th January

Having my hair done tomorrow. Curry. Tracey's favourite, today. My clothes reek. Dice still against me.

On washing-up, you can see straight across the dustbins and into the kitchen. Keeps himself to himself, that Gaspar. Thick lustrous hair you want to run your fingers through.

Alan was as bald as an egg. Didn't like being touched. Not even in the dark.

Special order came down. Doctors' conference. Twenty rounds of sarnies, twelve flasks of coffee, crockery, the lot. I can make sandwiches blindfold. I've loaded the trolley and I'm heading for the lift when Tracey – God knows where she'd been – steams through the swing doors and knocks me and the trolley for six. Flasks fly everywhere, noisy as skittles, fell two nurses and a porter, then skid along the corridor like seal pups on ice. Kitchen staff gawping, the Head Chef with his lollipop eyes … Miss Phillips scuttles back to her box of pills. Cher, who's still lurking about, retreats into the pantry, while I salvage what I can. Tracey, in shock and stockings ripped, is sent to First Aid where she passes out and so misses her lunch. Revenge is sweet.

Sunday 5th April

Three months since I last did this. We've been that busy. Unpacking the last box, I find this taped diary that I began back in January. So much has happened since then. Gaspar and I got talking, found we wanted the same things. And he's not shy, not at all. The old life's finished and I don't miss it.

Tracey got the boot when First Aid found she was on the wacky-backy. Dora's moved back to Brummy. And smelly Charlie's become a kitchen porter, God help them. Some college lass got Dora's job. But I reckon I came out on top. Straight up a magic ladder. Rolled a double six, I did. With mine and Gaspar's names on it. Sold my house and came out here. The café's almost ready, and it's a June wedding in Crete for us. No more snake days. Not ever.

****

A SPIDER IN A BOTTLE

It was cold in the hallway. Lucy watched the spider crawl along the window sill, hesitate, then turn in the direction of her hand where it rested beside the telephone. It wasn't a big spider, but big enough.

She wanted to do something about it but couldn't because of Omar's call being almost due. He rang her every Friday on the dot of six to get the cheap rate and to keep any disturbance to his evening's enjoyment at a minimum. He'd been quite frank about this.

The spider paused again, contemplating her thumb. Swiftly she moved her hand, her arm, finally her whole self, shifting the stool to the other side of the table. She didn't know which scared her most, the spider or the thought of having to kill it.

Puzzled, the creature sniffed the air, then turned and scurried towards her again. It was only inches away from her bare arm.

'Damn,' said Lucy under her breath, glancing at her wristwatch. Three minutes to six. She looked up and met the spider's eye. An involuntary shudder ran through her.

On impulse, she ran to the kitchen and hunted for some suitable container. There was an empty lemonade bottle sticking out of the pedal bin. That would do. She held the bottle against the wall, sliding it up beneath the creature's legs. Taken by surprise, he slipped into it. Just as she was screwing on the top, the telephone rang.

'You're coming this weekend? But I thought ...'

Changed his mind again. He'd always been good at that.

'But Tim's going to a birthday party tomorrow. Jason's his best friend.'

Yes, of course his father was more important. Lucy sighed. She would have to explain it to her son somehow. But even a five-year-old has a moral code. And a promise is a promise.

Replacing the receiver with a trembling hand, Lucy picked up the lemonade bottle and peered through its green glass. The spider was splashing about contentedly in a puddle of sweet liquid at the bottom. Plenty of air, she decided. He'd be all right for now. She shoved the bottle under the hall table and went upstairs to bath her son. There wouldn't be time to read him a story tonight. With a clear road, Omar would be here in an hour or so. And there was the meal to prepare yet. Omar was fussy about his food.

He arrived late, saying he'd already eaten. He was off-hand and irritable, embracing her roughly. They went straight upstairs to bed.

Afterwards, Lucy lay on her back listening to Omar's guttural snoring. His left arm was flung heavily across her belly, which kept rumbling with hunger. She supposed she had enjoyed their love-making, perfunctory though it had been. Too often, she felt he took her pleasure for granted. And not only with the bed thing.

At the beginning, before Tim was born, they'd been both lovers and friends, talking to each other and planning their future. But ever since he'd persuaded her, nearly four years ago now, to move into one of his country properties because 'it will be nicer for you, and for the child', their relationship had deteriorated.

Omar was quite rich, she realised, and his business going well. He paid all their bills, and it was a newish house, which he'd had lavishly furnished. Tim's school was only a ten-minute bus ride away. Her personal allowance more than covered all she wanted in the way of clothes and hairdos. But he'd refused point-blank to provide her with a car. Consequently, with only two buses a day into the nearest town, Lucy felt almost a prisoner. I'm like a Chinese concubine, she thought now, bringing up one of the Emperor's many children and keeping myself beautiful, ready for my lord when his fancy next turns to me. She recalled how her mother had advised against the relationship.

The next morning, Omar rose late and, after a leisurely bath, took his son out for the afternoon. Left to her own devices and still influenced by her thoughts during the night, Lucy came again to the green glass bottle hidden beneath the hall table. How safe the spider was in his warm world with all obtrusive sounds muffled. His own little glass house, proof against predators, with known space in which to roam and sweet sherbet to quench his thirst. But there was one thing which he lacked, which he surely wanted above all, and to which every creature on Earth has the right. His freedom.

Cradling the bottle, Lucy walked to the very end of the back garden, to the wild part where late bluebells reflected the sky and marigolds and trailing nasturtiums gashed the long grass with orange flames. There she knelt and almost reverently unscrewed the lid. She held the bottle horizontal that the spider might walk out with his pride intact.

The residual liquid was all gone and the inside of the green glass was spotted and misty with condensation. The spider did not walk out.

Lucy put her eye to the bottle's mouth. She could not see him. The bottle smelled yeasty and dank. Very carefully, she up-ended it where moss grew upon a low stone wall. And onto the green velvet a tiny, twisted, black twig fell.

Tenderly, she touched its back with one finger. It did not move. She sat beside it for a long time, thinking.

Omar, in spite of Tim's pleadings, would not stay for tea. There were some people he wanted to see, he said. Surprisingly, he failed to notice that Lucy made no effort to restrain him.

As soon as his car was out of sight, she filled a suitcase with clothes and essentials for herself and her son and collected all her personal papers from the bureau. Then she telephoned her mother briefly and rang for a taxi.

'Are you ready now?' asked the harassed radio operator.

'Yes,' Lucy answered with a smile, 'I am ready. Now.'

****

PARADISE

Sometimes Jacko dreams he has a different name, but his waking always erases it. These days he is reluctant to leave his bed, not only for its comfort and warmth. As for much of his life, his dream world is the kinder place.

This morning he rises early because someone called an assessor is due at nine. His bare feet skid on the thin mat which fails to insulate him against a cold, concrete floor. Automatically, he reaches under the pillow for his wallet and key, stuffs them into his trouser pocket. He was six months in this draughty, one-bed, ground-floor council flat before he stopped sleeping with his shoes, laces tied together, round his neck.

His shirt hangs on the back of a chair. That and the single divan are the only pieces of furniture in the room. He draws back the dingy curtains, rubs a circle of vision in the ice. Outside, cars swish by, buses snort as they pull away from the stop. On the far side of the valley, a white road snakes up to another hilltop where trees half conceal five tall buildings. He gazes longingly across this valley. The white road fascinates him. It makes his feet begin to itch again.

He shuffles into the narrow kitchen, flinches at sight of the bars outside his window. These bars are not to keep him in, but the kids' footballs out. He appreciates this but cannot control his reaction.

He takes his breakfast into the other room. Settled in the only armchair, an electric fire warming his legs and fresh bread and marge washed down with hot, sweet tea, he is happy. It is the best part of his day. Though his evening chats with Bill come a close second.

The letterbox rattles and something plops onto the lino. He guesses it's the minister's son doing deliveries before school. After washing up, he goes to the bathroom for his usuals, then retrieves the church magazine, recognising it by its cover illustration. He bins it without a second look.

Back in the kitchen he pours milk into a saucer and fills a bowl with cereals and seeds. Then he goes out the back, by the washing lines. Within minutes, a black cat sidles up to him.

'Hullo Cat,' he murmurs, fondling her willing head. 'Breakfast's ready.'

As her form slips thinly past him, his hand, slender and pale as a young girl's, runs the length of her rippling spine.

He strolls to where the yard merges with a stretch of scrub which belongs to no one. Beyond it, a copse conceals the edge of a land cliff. On this patch marigolds grow, and golden rod, chickweed, plantain and goosegrass. Even wild thyme. This is Jacko's pharmacy. Stooping, he gathers a bunch of plantain leaves. Then he scatters the cereal and seeds and waits, still as a tree. From the bushes, a shy nose sniffs the air. On an indrawn breath, Jacko produces a single whistle, vibrato, very high. And a red fox steps delicately forward to munch his free breakfast. For fully five minutes, a companionable silence enfolds them, then somewhere a door slams and the fox is gone.

'Hi, there.'

Jacko turns to face the bulky figure of his neighbour who is struggling forward on two sticks.

'Hi, Bill. Just off?'

'You coming?'

'No. Council man at nine. Can't leave you to move all on your own, can I?'

'You won't regret it. Everything's brand new up there. Radiators and showers and people to look after you when you get ill. Or too old.' He looks down at his once-strong legs. 'There's a clinic too.'

'And a caff?'

'We won't need cafes. Those flats are pure luxury, mate.' He swivels uncertainly. 'Gotta go now. Catch me bus. See you later.'

Jacko scoops up a couple of late windfalls and goes indoors. There's no sign of the black cat but the saucer is empty. He sets to work with dustpan and brush, then takes Vim to the washbasin in case the man needs to use the bathroom.

Somewhat to his surprise, the assessor turns out to be a young woman.

'Good morning, Mr. Robinson. I'm Bridget Allenson.' She flashes an identity card past him. He watches her warily as she settles on an upright chair, a sheaf of papers on her lap. Authority always scares him, but there's an openness in her manner which he finds calming.

'You'd like to transfer to Paradise Park, Mr. Robinson?'

'Yes – yes please,' he stammers.

'I note Mr. Buckley at Flat two is transferring also. You know him, do you?'

'Yes. We're good ... ' Friends seems too deep a word. 'Neighbours' he finishes.

She writes at length. Her brown hair is scragged back but one wisp escapes. Absent-mindedly, she tucks it behind her ear. Her fingernails are painted green.

'You received the booklet explaining everything? The different houses for different levels of dependence, etcetera?'

'I-er-lost it,' lies Jacko, knowing full well he'd binned it.

'Well, apart from Eden House, residents mostly look after themselves. As you do here,' she finishes brightly, her professional gaze encompassing the mean little room.

Jacko leans forward, flicks on the second bar of the electric fire. Bridget Allenson acknowledges the gesture by unfastening the top two buttons of her coat.

'Is it warm? There?'

'Heating's on day and night. October till April. All included.'

She turns over a page.

'You realise the rent's considerable higher?'

He stares at her. He's thinking how warm he'll be. And hot water from the taps. No struggling with kettles.

'Are you prepared to make up the difference?'

'Oh yes,' he says, not caring. He and Bill are going to live in a beautiful house in the woods. With no bars on the windows.

'As it happens, there's an unexpected third floor vacancy we could move you into. How about Friday?'

'Friday?' He's stunned, suddenly afraid. So long have his dreams kept him afloat. But when a dream comes true, you lose it, and have only reality to lean on. And reality, in Jacko's experience, could be hostile.

She's waiting, pen poised.

'Friday's all right.' He feels sick. 'Thank you,' he manages, remembering his manners.

She's passing a form to him, offering her pen. He's consumed with embarrassment, with terror. He falls back on the old lie. He's lost his glasses, can't see to read or write without them.

'Just do your best. I'll write the date.'

He scratches out the only three letters he's ever learned ... C O H. She looks keenly at him, but 'That's fine,' is all she says.

Once the front door has closed, Jacko goes to his kitchen where he pounds the plantain leaves to a pulp, then mixes in some Vaseline. This he takes to his friend the newsagent across the road who cut his hand rather badly the other day. In return he receives a twist of tobacco.

He is already perched on the back step, smoking a roll-up, when Bill returns.

'Great,' enthuses Bill when he hears the news. 'I'm moving in on Friday, too. Didn't say so before, in case – well, you know.'

It is quieter here than in the front where every shout, every thwack of ball resounds off the other blocks, and where dogs shit.

'Paradise here we come,' says Jacko, forcing it a bit, for dreams are fragile things.

'Too right,' says Bill, then changes the subject abruptly, like it had been no more than where to get a good deal on tobacco.

They relax onto their favourite subject. Bill has a worn roadmap which he spreads lovingly out, tracing routes with his stubby finger as he talks. Jacko listens, eyes closed. The piece of paper means nothing to him. He possesses a mental map of every last road in the country. They are his friends and he likes to recall adventures he has had on them. He misses them, longs to feel their history beneath his feet again.

Bill's finger takes him into Wales.

'Did you ever tramp round Dolgelly way, Jacko?'

'Many summers, when I was young. There was a girl from a gipsy family camped beneath the Cader. And a cottager in Arthog who gave me bread and cheese and beer. I drank it atop a mountain, on the old Roman road. Steep as a ladder it is. Up past the slate quarries.'

'What made you go to Wales?'

'The pull was always westward, away from the grime of London.'

'Ah, but she's kind to the likes of you and me in the winter, isn't she?'

'Yeah. Soup kitchens and shelters. Rowton House.'

'And the Salvation Army.'

'Oh, yes, of course, you got saved, didn't you?'

'Rescued. Victoria Embankment, Christmas Eve 1986. You?'

'Ran into this dog-collar, near Uffington. Car broken down. No idea where he was, poor bloke. Three miles to the nearest garage. Tossed me a fiver for directing him. Said if I was ever this way, to call on him. Four years ago, but his word held good. Got me into this flat. First time in my whole life – my own key to my own space.'

Bill is scribbling in a little notebook. Jacko talks on, eyes still closed. 'I'm not seventy even, but I'm worn out. Been on the road too long. Want to die in a bed, not in some derelict hole or wasted by a gang of murderous city yobs.'

Bill looks up from his writing.

'Uffington? Isn't there a white horse or something near there?'

'Old King Alfred's memorial to his victory over the Danes. A shepherd from Woolstone told me that.'

'Where were you born, Jacko?'

'Don't know.'

'Well, where'd you live when you were a kid?'

'Near a hill.'

'What hill?'

'Cotswolds, mebbe. Somewhere.'

'Not Wales?'

'That came later.'

Jacko sees again the stone cottage, its limestone tiles, and a green hill rising up behind. He hears Jenny, his dog, who is tethered to a post – her anguished yelps. He sees his mother at the door, weeping, and hears again his father's cold voice, and out in the lane an engine running ...

'You told me you ran away from home.'

'No. From *the* home. Someone left the garden door unlocked. I went in the clothes I stood up in. Just ran and ran. Didn't stop for miles. I'd been there twenty-one years.'

Jacko opens his eyes, sees the notebook.

'What you doing?'

‘I’m writing down your story. Everybody’s got a story to tell.’

‘My story’s mine.’

‘Sure, old fellow, sure.’ Bill pockets the notebook. ‘We both struck lucky though, finding benefactors. I mean, we’ve been accepted for Paradise Park with barely a question asked.’

His words make Jacko feel uneasy, but he’s not sure why.

More often now, Jacko’s early past is coming back to him. Sometimes in great, unwelcome chunks. So long as he was on the road, he could always outrun his memories, but now he’s stationary they’re catching up with him. He remembers his gentle mother in her lacy blouses, the tall, Nordic father who sent him to those hideous camps to ‘make a man of him’. He trembles, recalling the assault courses, his total ineptitude with weapons, the terror he could not hide on the rope-crossing of a gorge. All his muscles contract, yet it’s half a century ago.

‘I’m getting cold. Let’s put the kettle on,’ says Bill, stretching painfully. ‘This time next week, you’ll be sitting on your balcony.’

They grin at each other. A couple of old reprobates who have fallen on their feet.

It is Friday and Jacko has fed Cat, left food out for the fox, eaten his last apple. Now he waits patiently in the passage beside the meagre pile of his possessions. Bill and his furniture have already left.

‘I’ll see you later, then?’ Jacko had asked him.

'Sure,' said Bill, hobbling down the path for the last time. He'd turned, called back. 'I shall … I've enjoyed our talks.' And he was in the van and gone.

It is only when Jacko finally travels up the white road he's dreamed about so often, that he learns the reason for his friend's odd farewell. Bill is in Eden House, the one farthest away from Jacko. Eden has resident nurses and the people there mostly stay indoors because it's probably their last stop, explains the driver.

'You're dead lucky being rehoused up here,' he goes on.

'Why?'

'Council's clearing everyone out of your flats. For refurbishment, they call it. Most are going to huts on the old airfield. Really, it's just an excuse to charge higher rents. Only going to be one and two-bedroomed flats soon. Be a dam' sight quieter.'

Jacko can hear bridges crashing down behind him. No going back. He must make the best of this new life without Bill. It is only now, at the parting of their ways, that he realises just how much the friendship means to him.

It is several weeks later. The Christmas parties have come and gone, balloons all burst. It is January, a month of reckoning, for resolutions, for reality.

Jacko is sitting by the picture window determinedly counting his blessings. He is warm. These windows have never known ice. The warden visits him once a week but discourages him from going out. There are no buses here anyway. She is brisk, impersonal and reminds him of the matron who ruled his life for so long.

He attends games evenings, singsongs, but nothing dispels this almost physical weight he carries. It hangs on his shoulders like a heavy blanket, dragging him down. He's lonely for the lost companionship of Bill who he visits now and then. But their old camaraderie has gone. They no longer swap stories about roads, perhaps because Bill senses he's near the end of his. He talks little, waits for Jacko to leave.

He's missing Cat too, even the shy urban fox, and being able to use his knowledge of hedgerow plants. Some days he can hardly breathe here. He's having trouble sleeping and the clinic's little pink pills give him bad dreams and dopey days. Also, apart from the bathroom, there are no doors here, only room-dividers. He likes doors because he can choose how far to open them, what to let in, what to close himself off from. And another thing, his years on the road taught him never to sleep where there wasn't a second way out. You never know when the farmer or the police were going to turn up.

There's an ugly whirring sound outside. He goes onto the balcony. Where yesterday he watched squirrels shinning up and down trees, listened to birds, is now a gaping hole providing him with an unwanted, clear view of the industrial estate in the valley.

He feels physically ill. Is everything to be taken? He knows he is unpractised at asking for help. Besides, who would understand? Yet the idea that he might initiate change rasps like a match being struck in his darkness. It excites him. First, he'll order a taxi for Sunday. He strides across to the telephone.

It is Sunday, and Jacko is wedged in a corner pew waiting for the sermon to be over so he can ask his vicar friend for help. He doesn't want to lie about the luxury flats. Just to somehow explain that life in them is not for him. Will the man be angry at such ingratitude? How can he make him understand?

He is only half-listening to the sermon. Something about three wise men and life being a journey with mountains to climb. Apparently these men were rich, possessing every luxury but that wasn't enough. He can relate to that all right.

'Life is a voyage of discovery about others, about yourself too. Never let go of joy ....'

Well, he's certainly learned about himself these last weeks, thinks Jacko. But joy had been sacrificed. Something about these men returning to their own country. Yes, that's what he wants. And no way is an open-plan, high-rise apartment overlooking an industrial estate his country.

'Freedom is grounded in truth ....'.

Jacko resolves to be free again, preferably at ground level. He wants to be free to make friends with stray cats. Free to catch a bus. The choir are standing up, the vicar reaching his parting quotation.

'To thine own self be true, then nothing can touch you, not even the devil.'

And Jacko knows the man will understand. And the man does.

Somehow, Jacko isn't really surprised when, some weeks later, he's given the key to his old flat. But he is surprised when he walks into it. Newly decorated, heaters in every room, hot water, and a second armchair. Clean curtains at the windows too. And a new, thicker rug by his bed.

He fills a saucer with milk, then takes a handful of cereal and seeds out to the back area, perches on the step and waits.

A young girl with a baby on her hip sways out of the flat across the hall.

'You jes' moved in?' she calls.

'No,' smiles Jacko, 'I've come home.'

****

FAMILY TREE

The back garden was delightfully overgrown, scarlet nasturtiums snaking joyfully across both lawns, marigolds colonising once-immaculate herbaceous borders and wild borage and rough-necked alkanet peering through roses and lavenders.

Edward stepped carefully from the conservatory onto wet grass. Hearing the creaking of branches, he looked up to where the chestnut tree still towered over everything else. Glimpsed through a screen of leaves was Georgina perched side-saddle on their old swing, pushing gently with one elegant foot. For a fleeting moment, Edward thought how lovely yet fragile his sister appeared when she believed herself unobserved. He often considered it a shame that as soon as she became aware of another's presence her beauty seemed to flee.

'Careful,' he called,' those ropes don't look too good.'

'Old fusspot.' And she pushed herself higher. There was an ominous creaking and a shower of petals. Edward turned away, feigning interest in a tumbledown rockery. Very soon the creaking abated and she was strolling towards him.

‘Funeral went okay, didn’t it? Such a pretty little church.’ Her bright voice skimmed over the lawn, light as a dragonfly.

‘Yes.’ He knew he couldn’t talk about it. Guessed she’d bring up topic after topic until she got a dialogue going.

‘By the way Ed, thanks for ... we’ll pay you back. Things are a bit difficult right now.’

‘Forget it, kid.’ For god’s sake, he thought, what sort of a son couldn’t pay for his own mother’s funeral?

‘What on earth are we going to do with all her books? She’s got thousands of them, Ed?’

‘Mmm, some of the hardbacks may be worth a second look.’

‘Well, you’d know, wouldn’t you? Antiques and all that.’

They ambled round their childhood’s garden together, gathering memories like flowers, fresh now but soon to fade.

‘Look Ed, there’s that pond you pushed me into.’

‘I didn’t. You fell.’

‘You were always bigger than me.’

‘Hey, I’m five years older, remember.’

They gazed down at the pool’s still water, its dolphin fountain now no more than a dribble.

‘It’s all mucky. Slimy. Ugh.’ Georgina turned abruptly and headed towards the house.

‘I remember when it sparkled and splashed and goldfish darted about like wet flames,’ he murmured. ‘How you loved your garden, Mum. And how it loved you.’

‘What did you say, Ed?’

'Nothing.'

He was glad now that he had made the effort to visit last summer. Glad too that he'd found the grace to hear his mother's story. He turned once more to look at the chestnut tree his great-grandfather had planted, almost a hundred years ago, to mark his son's coming-of-age. Wasn't it said that wise men plant trees? Strange, but he felt that he would miss that tree more than he would miss the house.

Georgina was cleaning her shoes on a metal scraper by the step.

'You know, I can't understand why Mum never got herself another man. She never mentioned our father to us. It's like he was no more than a … a …' She kicked loose a clod of earth from one heel. 'I mean, would you have liked to go through your thirties without sex? I know I wouldn't.'

'You certainly didn't.'

'I made sure I had a good time.'

'How is Chet, by the way?'

'Okay.' Her tone was wary. 'He's got a new project and … our house is on the market.'

'Again?' He regretted it even as he said it. He knew how Chet's happy-go-lucky approach to life, especially to paying bills, was a constant worry for her.

'How's Dottie?' Typically, she changed the subject.

'Dorothy's fine, thanks.'

'Mandy still doing her gap year in Thailand? I must say I envy her living in Bangkok. A girl after my own heart.'

'I think she's working up country. In a village compound.'

'Oh. A good girl then.'

Inside the conservatory they flopped into basket chairs. Beyond the sliding glass, a blackbird plucked worms from the rain-soaked lawn. Edward, glancing at his sister's profile, noted the hardening lines, the tighter mouth. It must be difficult for her with Chet, he thought, an intelligent, charming entrepreneur who regarded riches or bankruptcy as all one big game. Not much security for a woman with children to care for.

Georgina rose, stretching languidly. 'Not very many at the funeral, were there? I thought we'd managed to contact everyone. Well, you did. You did tell everyone, didn't you, Ed?'

'Yes. Everyone in her address book, of course. And our family.'

'I wish I could remember what our father looked like. Do you remember him, Ed?'

'No. Not really,' he lied.

'You must remember him a bit. You were older. I was only a toddler.'

Edward was silent. He could remember very little of his father, who had died before his seventh birthday.

'He was … just a man. He was away more than at home. We didn't often see him.'

'Dark like me? Or fair like you?'

'Dark, I think,' he said, to comfort her.

'People who grow up with dads are so lucky. It's odd, I never really knew him yet I miss him.' She stood, nose pressed to the glass like a child at a toyshop window. Out on the lawn, two birds struggled for possession of a worm, neither letting go. 'In my dreams he's tall and handsome.

He can ride a horse, fly a plane, do anything. And he's always there for me, arms open wide … '

'I never minded not having a dad.'

'It was different for you. You had Mum.'

'So did you.'

'Not in the same way. She confided in you, pulled you up to her level. I was always her baby.'

'Maybe. But I just think that parents aren't that important once we leave home. It's nice to hear from them now and again, but they've done their job. We don't need them any longer.'

'I do.' Her voice was small, like a child's.

Edward thought again of his mother's admonitions throughout his childhood and beyond. 'Look after your sister, Ed. She's a fragile vessel.' He'd always done his best and would now. After last summer, he'd understood better why. Things he'd learned then he would never tell her. Let her keep her dreams. What good would reality do to her? She had enough of that in her life with Chet.

'Best make a start,' he said, rising from his chair.

She was still gazing out at the garden. It was raining again. A fine, steady rain with a bright sky beyond.

'How sad not to be able to come here again. Ever. So many memories.'

He knew it would be only too easy to comment that she'd only visited twice since young Blake was born. And he was at secondary school now. But to what end?

'Still,' she went on, 'I guess it'll fetch a good sum. Did she leave a will?'

‘Yes. Everything comes to us. But I’m afraid the house is mortgaged to the hilt.’

‘Oh.’ Her little girl voice again.

Edward knew that he too would be sorry to see the house go. He supposed he could just afford it, but without his mother there it would be merely another antique to add to his collection. There was no way Dorothy would ever consent to living so far from London.

They entered the wide, low-ceilinged room with its excess of reds and purples, its velvet covers, Eastern rugs, outrageous curtains. A faint smell of over-cooked roast dinner hung on the air. In one corner the baby grand nestled beneath a mound of papers. Georgina drew back the curtains.

‘Bet you can’t still play.’

‘Bet I can.’

He eased himself onto the bench where, aeons ago, he’d sat beside his mother, watching and learning. He remembered how her long fingers used to stroke music out of the keys. How she used to say, even last summer when he’d come up on impulse, ‘It’s all in there, Eddie, just waiting for you’.

He lifted the gleaming lid. The ivories felt warm. The second he touched them he sensed her presence, and the notes seemed to flow to meet him. Several bars in, he realised he was playing Chopin. A nocturne, one of her favourites. Three minutes later, he stopped in mid-phrase. Stood up. Walked away.

‘It needs tuning. It’s flat.’ He could not look at her.

Georgina slipped her arm through his, giving it a gentle squeeze. 'It's all right, Ed. We've still got each other. And our memories.'

He went over to the nearest bookcase, pulled out a book at random, flipping through its pages, seeing nothing.

'We could always employ a house-clearing firm?' she suggested.

'No.' The word fell, hard and heavy as a brick.

'No, I thought not. Well, let's get on with it, then. I've brought boxes and bags. If you do her books, I'll do her bedroom.'

He stood, listening to her light footsteps up the stairs, across the landing, into the room above his head. The room where he and his mother, this time last year, had talked long into the night. Each in a deep armchair, a single lamp burning low. And he'd finally understood about Georgina. Now, the book slipped from his fingers. Retrieving it, he saw that it was Proust, *'A la Recherche du Temps Perdue.'* In search of lost time, he murmured and, holding the book like a talisman, he settled in the rocking-chair where his mother's old blue shawl cushioned his back.

* * *

'They were sad times, ' his mother had begun, 'when you and Georgina were little.' Her flowing voice always used to make him think of a dark brown river curving its way to the sea. 'Bella's fiancé was nothing but trouble.'

'Bella?'

'My kid sister. Your Aunty Bell. You remember her, don't you?'

He'd thought he remembered. A soft lap to sit on, a tinkling laugh and stories told at bedtime. And some vague memory of sadness. Of tears maybe?

'Bella always got entangled with the wrong sort,' she continued, gazing down at the unlit fire. 'She was besotted with Joe, American Joe. He was a charmer. But unreliable. And' she paused, 'he had a temper.'

'You mean he was violent?'

'I'm afraid so. At times, very. It wasn't long after Georgina was born that Bella came running to us. We took her in, of course, her and the babe. Larry and me.'

'Larry?' He had to be sure. The past was so hazy.

'Your father.' She'd given him a long look then. 'Larry was a good man, Ed, and he loved you very much. Never doubt it.' She sighed. 'But he already had a wife in the States.'

'Where are they now, Aunty Bell and Joe? And my dad?'

'All gone. All long gone,' she sighed deeply. 'Larry and Joe were in the same unit, clearing minefields. They were killed within minutes of each other. It was a terrible shock for us both. But my poor dear Bella was totally distraught. You see, although she was afraid of him, she also loved him. She just never recovered. She died a year later, from pneumonia. Georgina stayed on with us of course. Eventually I adopted her. She was a nervous, frightened little two-year-old.'

The night gathered about them almost conspiratorially. Somewhere out beyond the garden, a fox had barked, and he'd thought then about how the past doesn't go away but is always there, influencing the present, the future. So Georgie was his cousin, not his sister. But it didn't make any difference, did it? They'd grown up together and his mother was, legally at least, her mother too.

'Being a single mother back then wasn't exactly easy, you know.' She had continued, her far-seeing eyes looking past him into a former life. 'Especially with two children. And Georgina was so difficult.'

He'd recalled bits of his teenage years. 'I was no angel, was I, Mum?' he'd said ruefully.

'You were just a boy. No trouble at all. An absolute doddle!'

And she'd laughed so generously that all the sorrow of the previous few minutes dissipated into thin air.

They'd gone on to talk of other matters. Edward, straining to remember his father could only recall a tall, fair figure on a motorbike who used to arrive and leave in a cloud of blue smoke. Like a magician.

'Was it Larry who taught me to climb the chestnut tree?' he'd asked her.

'Probably.' And she'd given him some photos. Five dog-eared black and white snapshots. 'We spent many happy hours under that tree, telling each other stories.'

'Was I there?'

'Later, yes. And your grandfather. On his good days.'

'A real family tree then?' he'd teased her.

'Oh, that old tree knows all our secrets. Father used to call it his treasure tree.'

'Why?'

'He never really explained.'

Edward then learned that his grandmother had been a great beauty, that his grandfather had showered her with jewels. That when she had died in childbirth, he never got over it. But that he had given Ed's mother her pearls. That his grandfather had been a rebel, not believing in paying taxes and the like. Especially not inheritance taxes.

'Went to prison once for that,' his mother had told him, with more than a little pride in her voice. Then, as Georgie might have done, she'd adroitly switched subjects. 'I trust you'll take care of my lovely baby grand piano?'

'When?'

'When I die, you silly boy.'

He hadn't known what to say. His mother had always been there. He hadn't even begun to think of her as getting old, let alone dying. He'd forced himself to acknowledge the loose skin of her throat, the puckering of her chin and the dips in her cheeks which were hollows, not dimples.

'You do still play, I hope?'

'Of course. I love it.'

'It belonged to your great-grandfather. It possesses almost as many secrets as the chestnut tree.'

'Did Grandfather play?

'No. It was your grandmother who was the musical one.'

* * *

Edward stirred himself. He'd been daydreaming and had barely started on the books, let alone the furniture. Already he heard Georgina's light step on the stairs. Quickly, he gathered an armful of books, depositing them on the table.

'Ed! You've hardly started! I've nearly finished upstairs. I'm leaving bagfuls of stuff in the hall. You must help me with the heavier things. But first I'm going to make us some coffee.'

'Good idea.' He began seriously to sort some books. The paperbacks he'd take to the nearest charity shop. But he knew he'd find it difficult to give away any of the hardbacks. He'd have to sell the house. If only it were not mortgaged. Georgie's share of the sale would have given her financial independence from the spendthrift Chet. Life was full of might-have-beens.

He strolled over to the piano, strummed a few phrases. He enjoyed playing medleys, the subtle changes of key. He resisted the lure of fresh coffee from the kitchen only because he felt there was something he ought to remember. Something his mother had said about the piano.

Georgina entered with two mugs of steaming coffee. 'Why don't you play a proper tune? Something cheerful? There's sure to be some sheet music somewhere.'

'Mum played by ear. And Grandfather couldn't play at all.'

'What's that then, sticking out from the top?'

He propped open the grand piano's top and, from its dusty interior, drew out a flimsy sheet of paper. Brown with age, its curled edges crumbled like autumn leaves.

'There's handwriting … look. And I know the song, don't you?' She began to sing, suiting actions to her words.

He could just decipher it. 'For my grandson, Edward, He who seeks, finds.' Finds what? Memory of his mother's words mingled with questions in his head. Something about the piano having almost as many secrets as the tree? Why did she only have the pearls? He'd already decided on his next action when his sister's brittle soprano delivered with a flourish the song's last line.

' … beneath the spreading chestnut tree! What's up, Ed? Why are you looking like that?'

'Come on, kid, we're going treasure-hunting. Follow me.'

Giggling like a couple of kids, they stepped once more into the singing garden, the sun now hot on their backs. As they ran, they exchanged looks, laughed, and the years fell away like notes of music dying. Edward paused briefly to grab a spade from the potting shed.

At the base of his grandfather's treasure tree, he began to dig. And there, in a satin-lined silver box, were their grandmother's jewels. Sparkling sapphires, rubies, emeralds, more pearls, little drops of moonlight, and diamonds running through Georgina's fingers like a stream of rainbows. At last, thought Edward, she'll be safe. And his heart filled with love and gratitude for the old man. His rich, rebellious grandfather.

****

TWO'S COMPANY

'I never knew why she left me.' John's tone is baffled rather than plaintive. 'I thought she was happy. I was.'

'Over a year now.' Denise observes him warily. 'Lot of water under the bridge, eh?'

'Pity you and I lost touch as well. Where was that teaching job? Spain?'

'Portugal. Didn't work out.' She sips red wine, glances again towards the door.

'I'm sorry.' He tips his bottle of Budweiser. 'Remember Camberwell? Us being the 'terrible trio'?

We did everything together, much of it bad!'

'Yeah, Lyn and me, and you. Another time, another place.'

Behind the bar, someone drops a tray of glasses.

'Right John, you got anyone now?' She laughs uncertainly.

'No chance. It's Lyn or no one for me.'

'You care that much? I hadn't realised … I thought … Lyn said there were quarrels.'

‘She was so impatient to start a family but we were both broke. Now, of course, with my lectureship ... how about you? Anyone special yet?’

‘Sort of, yes, that is – I thought so, but she’s still in love with ... ‘

A sudden draft of cold air wafts over them as the door swings open.

‘Oh, there you are, Den,’ Lyn hesitates.

Denise has risen and they embrace briefly.

‘Look who’s here, Lyn,’ Denise pushes her into the seat opposite John. ‘Tell Lyn your good news.’

She backs towards the door, realising they have eyes only for each other. The door closes behind her with a soft, relinquishing sigh.

****

THE SHELL

I never knew why she left it behind. Such a beautiful object. I have it still but dare not use it.

We met by accident one September day on the deserted promenade in the teeth of a westerly gale. I, a lost sailor seeking harbour, she, a stranded adventuress. Huge waves drove far up the beach, throwing the sea's detritus onto the path beyond. She was blown towards me, a long blue skirt billowing round her, totally concealing her feet, her golden hair an unfettered cascade. She handled her wheelchair with consummate ease.

We soon fell into easy conversation. I loved her tales of travel, of distant islands she knew. She spoke of seas like old friends. 'The Indian's a kind fellow but the North, he is cold.' When I mentioned my sailing round the Hebrides, her melodious voice grew dreamier still. 'Ah, the home of seals, and of seal men,' she sighed. I asked about the conch shell she carried in her lap.

Reluctantly she blew it and I felt lifted into another dimension. The seagulls went crazy and the ocean heaved as if giving birth.

The autumn solstice brought fresh storms. She revelled in the rain. One morning, struggling against the wind, I glimpsed her down on the shoreline, heard again the conch shell's cry, watched as his arms reached out from a rolling wave to clasp her. With a flick of rainbow fins they disappeared together. Her wheelchair lay askew, the huge shell beside it.

****

WOLVES SINGING

The wolves are singing again. Melinda strokes aside a drift of muslin so I can see the stars. The fields glisten like powdered glass. Starlight shades the sky into darkest blue. Mazarine blue. That's such a lovely sounding word. Their song echoes from far over the hills. It is filtered by the forest. Hollow contralto phrases alternately fan out then fold in. A series of controlled glottal stops as smooth as pebbles in a fast-flowing stream. How do they do it? With their tongues? Or their throats?

'How should I know?' Melinda does not look at me. She's busy tying back drapes so the whole window is open for me.

'It came upon the midnight clear, That glorious song of old' ... Boys' voices. Perhaps it's from Kings' College on the world service. Or is it in my head? No. It must be the radio. 'Of angels bending near the earth, To touch their harps of gold ...'

Ah, angels! If I look really hard, would I see them? Their vast, white wings shouldering constellations, immaculate fingers plucking golden strings. The vibrations flicking the air out of place in a zillion microscopic patches. Like the music of the spheres? To be heard only once and all other music thereafter to clang like tuneless cowbells?

Leo says this is a myth. Damn his realistic, scientific mind. Melinda brings the radio into my room. She places it beside my bed, plugs it into the wall. She has to remove my bedside light in order to do this. Leo has taken all our adaptors for his efforts with the fairy lights in the hall. Melinda hopes I'll be well enough to join in the carols round the Christmas tree. Some children are coming up from the village. My ex-pupils. Or perhaps the offspring of my ex-pupils. I lose track of time.

A young wolf got separated from his pack the other evening. We heard his solitary cry over and over again. It was followed by distant howls across the snow. A wolf's call can be heard as much as ten miles away. And each wolf has his own individual voice, just as we do. *Canus lupus pambasileus*, a sub-species of the grey wolf, I am told. They live for ten or twelve years.

Leo calls from where he is decorating the tree and Melinda goes out to him without first switching on the radio for me. I lean precariously out of bed to reach the wall point and in so doing, knock over the lamp which crashes to the floor. Seconds later, Melinda hurries back into my room, adjusting her hair.

'Oh, Ben, what have you done?' she says in that half-mocking, half-scolding way she's adopted since I became confined to my bed.

She looks flustered, slightly annoyed, though not, I think, with me. Together we heave my carcass back under the blankets. Then she kneels down to fix things. The radio comes on and a treble is singing solo … 'Silent night, holy night, all is calm, all is bright...' My hand hovers above her dark curls. I want to touch them, feel them move through my fingers like beads of velvet. But I know what she'd say. Just in time, I burrow my hand into the anonymity of the bedclothes.

A thread of perfume hangs on the air as she leaves. Chanel No. 5. And something else. My nostrils stretch wide to scoop the edge of it before it dissipates. Tobacco. Strong. That black, French stuff. Yes, Leo rolls his own. We each choose our own poison. I've a secret store of mine which Melinda hasn't found yet. It's at the back of the drawer behind the socks I no longer wear. It's comforting to think of it hidden there, waiting for me. I'm saving it for a special occasion when I'll enjoy one last, forbidden swig.

Each wolf pack marks out scent routes covering the whole of its territory which can be as much as 5,000 square miles. These make a pattern as complicated as any inner-city road or rail map. These tracks remain the same as long as that pack continues to control that stretch of land. A wolf's sense of smell is ten times as sensitive as that of a man. Wolves can sense the weakness of a creature from more than ten miles away and will never let up once they are on the trail.

They hunted early this morning. I heard them. And they must have got a kill for they've been silent all afternoon. Now, when the moon is high and hangs like a paper hoop in the blue ink sky, they sing.

Leo says I'm losing it. That wolves either bark or howl and do not make any sound which is purely for pleasure.

Hence, he says, they do not sing. He is a scientist and knows such things. Melinda says nothing. Perhaps she remembers the nights she and I walked through the snow, wrapped to our cheeks in furs, down to the river. It was frozen solid for a yard or more from either bank and there was just this narrow channel of grey-green water folding and unfolding itself in long fluted waves that ran with the current.

She used to put her gloved hand in my pocket for extra warmth. Her hand was warm against my thigh. Sometimes the air was so cold that our noses crackled when we laughed. Her eyes shone, deep brown pools.

Memories of our days together. Each memory sits clear and separate as a painting on a gallery wall. I walk from one to the next, pausing longer at some, to experience again a flash of emotion, a provocative glance, the touch of her, the scent of her.

On other days, the memories all jumble up as if some kid's run through the gallery ripping pictures off the walls, throwing them in a heap on the floor. Then I call for her on some pretext or other, just so I can see and hear her as she is now. In the present. And thus create a new memory, albeit only a swift sketch. But it's fresh and reassuring. And once she's here with me, I can sleep. No problem. No need of an injection either. Blessed oblivion.

Summer days with Melinda were the best. She complains I was always away. But I was never away for one second longer than I had to be. The tours were the worst. Three months in Europe. Two in South America. If you sing with a company you've not much choice. I explained at the beginning how it wouldn't always be so. How I'd get to be principal and could pick and choose my roles more. Then I could earn enough in the winter to spend all summer with her here in the north. And I would have done. Only one more year. Then this. Out of the blue. Threatening everything, ruining everything. Why me? I'm told they all ask that. I scream it silently each morning I wake in this narrow bed. Why me? Why? Why? Why?

This question has become superfluous, like so many other unanswered questions. Reasons don't matter anymore. Things are as they are and we must make the best of them.

Doc McLure came this morning. In his black bag sat my newest lover, lady morphine. I stroked her cool glass phial before he pumped her into me. Her juice spread, swirling, smooth as cream, coating every raw spot with velvet. I drifted in a post-coital dream. I didn't hear him leave, but thought I caught the tail-end of a whispered exchange between he and Melinda.

Leo was out with the dogs. I notice he avoids meeting the doctor. I guess he's being tactful. As he has always tried to be. I'm glad he's staying on for a bit. Melinda deserves better company than the sick old man I have become. Leo is a dependable guy. It's a comfort to know that he will come if she needs him. No comprehension of music of course. Tone deaf, apparently. Shame. For Melinda has song in her. But at least her silent brushes create arpeggios on canvas.

The wolves are silent still. I miss their calls. Especially that lone wolf. Melinda closes the shutters, covers them with drapes. To keep out the dark? 'No,' she answers sharply, 'to keep out the cold.' But she is too late for the cold is inside me, a small tight knot of it, a snowball somewhere in my middle and spreading.

I cannot sleep. I call and Melinda comes running. It's only eight o'clock but she's already in her night things. With difficulty, I shift my carcass and she lays herself down beside me. Awkwardly, my arm goes round her and suddenly we are hugging and she is crying, sobbing silently into my neck. My fingers fondle her curls. She does not pull away. I am so happy I want to die now, this moment. There, I've thought the forbidden word. The thing we do not mention.

The children came. Was it only yesterday? Leo has transformed our living-room into an Aladdin's cave. Coloured lights everywhere. Melinda was determined I should be there when they sang round the tree. Doc brought a wheelchair and he and Leo heaved me into it. Propped up, pumped up with Lady M, tucked up in a huge scarlet blanket with my beard hanging over it, I played the part of Santa Claus. In a dream almost, I doled out gifts from a sack Melinda placed beside me. The children's voices were divine, so pure. My ex-pupils, my little music-makers. Go on singing and you will survive in this wicked, old world.

Leo's gone away. Melinda won't say why or for how long. Did my little outburst on Christmas Day do it? The wolves were circling, quite close. He set off with a rifle. I sent Melinda after him, to beg on their behalf. How low can I sink? I shouted at her. She cried. I cried. But she went and there was no shooting. And the wolves are back. But Leo has gone.

Melinda is unhappy. I cannot bear to see her like this. She wanders about the place aimlessly, bereft. This won't do. It won't do at all. Doc has plastered Lady M to my side. All I have to do is press a little button and she is all mine.

Melinda watches me from behind her eyes. Her anxiety hangs like smoke on the air. It's nearly time and I have things to do. At last, two long phone calls and she runs in to say Leo will be back on Friday. Three days. In my dreams, I call him, will him to return, my lone wolf. I cannot do it without him.

It's New Year's Eve and Melinda hums as she irons sheets and flicks a duster round. She walks the dogs and comes home flushed and beautiful but annoyed to have left her mobile on my bedside table. Its memory is overflowing with texts. Hers were warm honey running through the ether. Her vocabulary has not changed. His were almost prim in comparison. But then he is a scientist, as he frequently points out.

New Year's Day and he's back! I heard him last night, quite close. A single howl. A new year, a new page in the book of life. Melinda's baked a special cake. She tried to feed me a slice. It was gravel in my dry mouth. Another year on this dying planet spinning in space? I don't think so. It'd be almost indecent. I'm rapidly becoming more cadaver and less man. 'Don't talk like that,' she cries, tears not far. But it's true. Finally, after numerous reassurances that I'll be okay here alone, she leaves for the airport to pick up Leo. At last.

Rolling out of bed is laughable. Am festooned like the Christmas tree. Wires everywhere. Most pop out of their own accord. The needle is like extracting a long splinter. I lean on the chest, pull out the drawer, fumble amongst the balls of socks. I grasp my old love by her amber neck, break her open and take in a long draught of her. She fills my mouth, burns my throat and I'm gasping with relief at reaching an oasis in my year-long desert.

I tuck her into my dressing-gown pocket, somehow get shoes on my feet. Proper clothes are out of the question. The blanket will suffice. Lady M nudges me and together we totter to the door and open it.

It is bright moonlight. Blue-tinged snow turns the land into a moonscape. Shapes are unrecognizable. A little hill just where the forest begins, and there he stands. *Canus lupus*. He's nearly three foot tall. He's enormous, must weigh 170 lbs or more. No doubt the dominant male. So only he will mate this year. He could travel as much as three hundred miles to find her. He'll court his bitch in January, get her with pup in February. A superb creature. He looks at me warily. I stumble towards him.

Dear God, but it's cold. He howls and I stop in my tracks. An echoing howl sounds very far off. I drag my recalcitrant body slowly up the hill, swigging whisky as I go. I fall at his feet. He does not move. I take as deep a breath as I can and begin to sing. Two bars into my favourite aria and he howls again. Our voices spiral round each other, notes bounding across the empty snowfields. We sing together, to the new moon, the new year, new life.

The cold outside is rapidly converging on and joining up with the cold inside me. I am so very tired. I curl up on the snow, snuggling into my scarlet blanket. The grey wolf is still singing. It all feels familiar somehow, and safe. Like coming home. I feel his warm breath as he licks my cheek. I am a child again, in my cot, its feather quilt enfolding me. Above me, the skylight with its map of stars. I am home. My eyelids close. I will sleep now.

****